MW01138804

MURDER & MEGA MILLIONS

A High Desert Cozy Mystery - Book 6

BY

DIANNE HARMAN

Copyright © 2018 Dianne Harman

All rights reserved, including the right to reproduce this book, or portions thereof, in any form without written permission except for the use of brief quotations embodied in critical articles and reviews.

Published by: Dianne Harman
www.dianneharman.com

Interior, cover design and website by
Vivek Rajan

This is a work of fiction. Names, characters, places, and incidents either are the product of the author's imagination or are used fictitiously, and any resemblance to actual persons, living or dead, business establishments, events, or locales, is entirely coincidental.

ISBN: 978-1986668415

CONTENTS

ACKNOWLEDGMENTS

The first question I'm asked after I meet someone and they find out how many books I've written is, "How do you keep coming up with ideas?"

It's hard for me to answer, because ideas come from everywhere – a person I meet, a phrase, or perhaps something I read. This book is certainly a case in point. A few months ago my husband came home from playing golf and told me about a woman who had joined his threesome on the golf course. He said he was quite surprised when he asked her if she had a career, and she told him she was a philanthropist.

It stayed with me, because I've never met anyone who defined themselves by using that word, and so a book was born. I decided I'd write a book with one of the characters being a philanthropist. The inclusion of art and antiques in the book came about quite naturally to me, as I love and collect both of them.

Recently my husband and I were staying at the La Quinta Resort in Palm Springs while I was preparing to write this book. One morning I wandered over to the coffee shop and discovered some beautiful pieces of art hanging on the wall, all of which depicted scenes from in and around the beautiful La Quinta Resort. I immediately thought one of the paintings would make a great cover for this book.

It just so happened that the artist responsible for these beautiful pieces of art, John W. Flanigan, was in the coffee shop. I got to talking to him and learned that he's the resident artist at La Quinta. I commented that I was an author and would love to use one of his paintings on the cover of a future book. He agreed to my request, gave me his business card with his Instagram address, which is @jwflanigan, and told me all of his art is displayed on the Instagram site.

Unfortunately when I tried to copy one of his paintings off of Instagram for use on the book cover, I learned I couldn't use it because of Instagram's policies. I had to develop a different cover which I think turned out vry well, but I still wish I could have used one of John's paintings. They are so beautiful!

To Vivek, Tom, and Connie, many thanks for taking care of the details and allowing me to do the broad strokes! And to my loyal readers, thank you for your buys, your borrows, your reviews, and your emails.

And as always, I hope you enjoy the read as much as I enjoyed the write!

Win FREE Paperbacks every week!

Go to www.dianneharman.com/freepaperback.html and get your FREE copies of Dianne's books and favorite recipes immediately by signing up for her newsletter.

Once you've signed up for her newsletter you're eligible to win three paperbacks. One lucky winner is picked every week. Hurry before the offer ends!

PROLOGUE

The sounds of traffic rushing through Four Corners, California, where Highways 395 and 58 intersect, woke twelve-year-old Melissa up on that windy winter morning. Four Corners wasn't an exciting place to live, but it was the only place she knew. Surrounded by love, Melissa may have had little in the way of material things, but she was happy and content. She rolled over in bed, stealing a few more minutes of warmth under the tattered and worn blankets that covered her bed. If she'd known in a few hours her life would be changed forever, she would have stayed in bed far longer.

She also didn't know that in years to come she'd become rich beyond her wildest dreams and then get murdered.

Karma? Fate? Or destiny? None of us can tell what the future holds, nor did she.

CHAPTER ONE

Melissa Ross hated the wind that always swirled around the gas station her father owned at the intersection of the two highways that ran through Four Corners. She knew both highways led somewhere else, but being only twelve years old, she didn't know where. She guessed it had to be somewhere much more glamorous and beautiful than the dry, hot, sunbaked desert that surrounded Four Corners. The two highways that intersected at Four Corners, 395 running north and south, and 58 from east to west, were heavily traveled by cars and trucks.

The trucks drove fast, and the cars drove even faster. She was sure they wanted to drive as fast as possible, so they could get to some place where people didn't have to listen to the incessant sounds of the traffic and wind. No one wanted to stop at Four Corners unless they needed gas.

Her mother, Ellen, had often told her about those places. They were towns and cities that had museums, antiques, and art - all the things her mother loved. She and her mother spent hours looking at the art and antique magazines Ellen subscribed to.

Looking at the magazines was the only thing they could do to escape the constant sounds of the incessant traffic on the highway. Cars and trucks frequently stopped at their gas station while they were on their way to another part of the state. Each time a big rig shuddered to a stop, their tiny apartment behind the station shuddered as well. Her mother promised her that someday they'd leave and get to see all the wonderful things they'd seen in the magazines.

Ellen's eyes lit up when she talked about the trips they would take. Melissa didn't care about the destination as much as she wanted to be part of something that made her mother happy. The rest of the time, when the dog-eared magazines went back to their place on the cluttered shelf in the tiny kitchen, the shining light in Ellen's eyes went out.

A few months earlier her mother had finally persuaded her father to buy a computer. Despite her father's protestations, he'd relented, and her mother spent hours on it, with Melissa by her side, looking at museum sites, auction results, and antiques. The faint traces of a smile crossed Ellen's face as they explored the art world online, every click transporting them farther away from the dust and grime of Four Corners.

"Someday, Melissa, someday," Ellen would say, guiding her daughter's hand as it rolled the computer mouse across the mouse pad, and together they traveled the globe with it.

Someday never came for Ellen. When the San Bernardino deputy sheriff came to the gas station that morning, along with a man from the county coroner's office, Melissa knew that something bad had happened to her mother. She tried to go into her parents' bedroom, but her father told Melissa and Ed, her older brother, to stay in Melissa's room. It was the first time she'd ever seen her father cry, but not the last.

Later, after her father called a couple of men he knew to take over the gas station for the day, he'd come into Melissa's bedroom where she and Ed were sitting on the bed. He'd sat down between them and taken their hands in his.

"Children, somethin' bad's happened," he said gulping for air and wiping a tear from his cheek with the back of his hand. "No use sugarcoatin' this. You'll find out soon enuf'. It'll be the talk 'round these parts for a while. Yer' mom couldn't go on livin' here. Always promised her I'd take her to a big town when I made enuf' money. Didn't happen," he said, openly sobbing, his thin body racked with grief.

He caught his breath and continued. "She couldn't take it no more and took a whole bottle of them pills the doctor in Barstow gave her for depression. At least she didn't suffer. Musta' taken 'em when I was out gassin' up the truck early this mornin'. Came in to get me some breakfast 'bout the time I always do. There weren't no breakfast. I went into our bedroom, and that's when I found her. She weren't breathing and was white as the sheet she was layin' on. I called 911."

Melissa sat in silence, holding her father's hand, and watching the tears roll down his face.

Ed was the first to speak. "Dad, what're we gonna' do now?"

"Son, we still got each other. We'll jes' have to work this out." He put one arm around each of them, pulling them close. Ed pushed his arm away and stormed out of the room.

Working it out had lasted for almost a year before Melissa's father gave in to his grief and didn't wake up one morning, leaving Melissa and Ed to work it out for themselves.

*****

Now, several years later, Melissa looked out the cracked window of her uncle's home, if one could call a three-room tarpaper shack a home. She could see the desert town of Barstow in the distance. To the east stretched miles and miles of the desolate Mojave Desert. To the west, she knew, about 150 miles away, was Los Angeles and the Pacific Ocean.

The years since her father's death had not been easy. Her uncle, Christopher Ross, had made it very clear from the beginning that the only reason he'd taken in his brother's two children when his brother had died was because there were no other relatives.

He spent his time sprawled on the couch watching television, drinking beer, going to the Quick 'N Go to buy more beer, and going to the mailbox down on the highway once a month to get the disability check the oil company paid him for being injured when he was working for them on an oil rig near Barstow.

The word her mother had used so often, "someday," had become a mantra to her, and Melissa had vowed the moment her mother died, that someday she would do what her mother never could, buy the art and antiques Ellen had always so desperately yearned for. She had no idea how it would happen, but she knew it would.

Melissa was seventeen when she'd finally saved enough money from her job at the café down the road to leave her uncle and the tarpaper shack that had become her home.

Her brother had joined the Barstow branch of the East Side Victoria gang and had left two years earlier. She'd never heard from him again and wondered from time to time if he was even still alive. Melissa knew the young men in that gang had a very short life span, in or out of prison.

She carefully put the few clothes she owned, and the worn copy of the Art and Antiques magazine she and her mother had been looking at the day before she died, in her backpack. She tiptoed quietly past her uncle who was snoring on the grimy grey couch and walked out the door, stepping into a new life.

CHAPTER TWO

"Thank you, Percy," Rhonda Taylor said to the driver from her seat in the back of the car, as he expertly pulled her Bentley into the long, curved driveway. He got out of the car and walked around to the backseat door, opening it for her. She quickly got out and walked up the steps of her large Mediterranean-style home located in the original part of Palm Springs.

Rhonda's home was one of the largest and most expensive in the area. The red-tiled roof topped the L-shaped southwestern style home which surrounded an Olympic size swimming pool. Not that Rhonda ever swam. The only time her hair ever touched water was at the beauty salon. Beyond the pool was a pool house and two guest houses. One side of the house was set snugly up against the Santa Rosa mountains. Rhonda's husband, Dr. Wesley Taylor, a prominent psychiatrist and the head of the psychiatric department at the nearby Eisenhower Medical Center in Rancho Mirage, was a scratch golfer and often invited doctors he met at various conferences to play golf with him and stay in one of the guest houses.

Between his medical practice and his golf, Dr. Taylor didn't spend much time with Rhonda. Rhonda was pretty sure that in addition to his patients and golf, he indulged in his fascination with beautiful women. It was no secret among the medical community that Dr. Taylor's good friend, Dr. Lewis, a plastic surgeon, was more than happy to provide Dr. Taylor with a never-ending supply of beautiful women. It had been rumored for many years that part of Dr. Lewis' post-surgery procedures included lowering his fees for women who were amenable to getting to know Dr. Taylor in an intimate way.

This being Palm Springs, where looks are everything, and plastic surgery is considered nothing more than routine body maintenance, Dr. Taylor always had a fresh supply of women to choose from. Long ago, Rhonda and her husband had arrived at an unwritten agreement which consisted of her ignoring his "long hours" in return for him giving her free rein to indulge in her passion – that of being the most prominent collector of art and antiques in the Coachella Valley. This was no mean feat given the amount of money available to a large number of the wealthy local residents, who also had a passion for art and antiques, but Rhonda was quite pleased that she alone reigned supreme.

At least she had been until a woman by the name of Melissa Ross started buying art and antiques. And buy she had, with wanton abandon. The Ross woman had personally been responsible for driving up certain areas of the art and antique market in the United States. Unfortunately, these were the same areas that Rhonda had lorded over for many years, primarily fine art of the early 20th century as well as California pottery and living in Palm Springs, of course, Native American baskets, rugs, and pottery. It seemed like these days everywhere she went someone mentioned that Melissa Ross had bought this or that.

Rhonda had never met the woman and had no desire to, because she was afraid she'd do or say something she'd really regret. However, what had happened at the auction in Los Angeles earlier that evening made her decide something had to be done to put the Ross woman out of commission.

Rhonda had met the man who placed her bids, Jerry Mason, at Bonham's Auction House in Los Angeles. Although everyone in the California auction world knew who she was, she preferred to let him bid for her. She'd talked to him earlier in the day and given him a list of the lots she wanted him to bid on as well as the top price she was willing to pay for any given item.

She'd eagerly looked forward to tonight's auction because a painting by her favorite artist, Granville Redmond, had been added at the last minute to the items that were scheduled to be sold. Rhonda secretly paid one of the staff at Bonham's well for information such as that and had high hopes that none of the other California art collectors would know about the late addition.

The desired result was for her to be able to purchase the painting at a fraction of what it would bring if it had been publicly featured in the auction sale catalog. Her contact at Bonham's told her the owner desperately needed money for an expensive surgery for her granddaughter and the only way she could get that kind of money that fast was to part with her beloved painting.

In addition to the Granville Redmond painting, there were several pottery pieces and baskets attributed to California Native American tribes which Rhonda planned on adding to her collection, along with a spectacular piece of Catalina Island pottery, a round tray. Although she had a number of pieces of Catalina pottery, she had yet to possess anything as well done as the piece displayed in the auction catalog. It was round with a blue and white glaze, depicting a three-masted sailing ship on the ocean set against a background of a blue sky.

The auction had been a disaster from the very beginning. There was a San Francisco simulcast and as soon as it began and the camera panned over the San Francisco bidders, Jerry leaned over and whispered in her ear, "Melissa Ross is represented. There's the guy who always bids for her, Clayton West." He nodded towards the screen and Rhonda felt her stomach knot up.

Two hours later she felt like throwing up. Clayton West had outbid Jerry on every single piece she'd wanted. To add insult to injury, in order to ensure that Melissa Ross would get the Granville Redmond California poppy painting, Clayton had raised Jerry's bid by $25,000, rather than the $5,000 increment being requested by the auctioneer. Wide-eyed, Jerry had looked over at Rhonda to see if she wanted to outbid him. Rhonda was in a state of shock and simply shook her head, indicating he wasn't to bid anymore. As the auctioneer hammered his gavel down and said, "Sold," the camera panned on Clayton West, who was smiling broadly.

Rhonda didn't even bother to say goodbye to Jerry as she furiously strode up the aisle of the auction house and out the door. When she got outside she opened the door of the Bentley before Percy could even get out of the car and open it for her.

"Home, madam?" he asked.

"Yes, and as fast as you can get there," she snapped back, her face twisted in fury.

*****

Rhonda felt like she'd been hit by a truck. The reputation she'd so carefully crafted over the years as being the foremost collector of California art had just come to a crushing, and yes, embarrassing end. She'd fully expected to see a photo of the painting by Granville Redmond featured in the Desert Sun newspaper the following day with the caption "Just Purchased by Palm Springs' Leading Art Collector" or some such similar thing, and without mentioning her name, everyone would know it had been Rhonda Taylor that the caption was referring to.

Instead, her days as a leading California art connoisseur had come to a screeching halt with the sale of the painting, not to mention the Catalina pottery piece Rhonda had coveted, to that dreadful Ross woman. Building a reputation as the preeminent Palm Springs, California art collector had been Rhonda's goal when she came to the realization shortly after her marriage that her husband had other interests in mind such as golf, medicine, and other women.

Having a loving marriage was definitely not part of his plan, and theirs had become a marriage of convenience. What was convenient for his wife was that Dr. Wesley Taylor was not only a wealthy man in his own right, but he'd inherited a great deal of money from his father, who had been a cardiologist in Palm Springs.

Some contracts require attorneys. Some contracts require in-depth conversations between the parties. The Taylor contract only required a pretense – that the marriage was good. This left both parties free to do whatever they wanted. It had worked out well for many years. Wesley had his lady friends, and Rhonda was the queen of the Palm Springs art world. However, this arrangement was dramatically upset when Melissa Ross arrived on the scene. Not only was Rhonda no longer the foremost art collector in Palm Springs, she'd been humiliated and was certain she was now the laughingstock of the Palm Springs art community.

She was convinced she had to take some sort of dramatic action to regain her coveted position in the local art community. It was obvious she couldn't outbid her opponent, so she'd have to get rid of her. It was really quite simple.

No one would ever suspect that the leading psychiatrist in Palm Springs was married to a woman who was capable of committing murder, but that was all the better for Rhonda's plan.

The upcoming art auction in Palm Springs would be the prelude to the main event, Melissa Ross' murder. The heirs of an elderly Palm Springs couple had decided to place their California art collection with an auction house rather than sell it themselves. Rhonda had been interested in several pieces, and since it was taking place in Palm Springs, Rhonda was sure Melissa would also be attending. Too bad Melissa wouldn't be able to enjoy the pieces she'd buy at the auction.

As a doctor, Rhonda's husband often used the phrase "When someone's time has come, there's nothing that can be done." She thought it was rather fitting for Melissa, the only difference being that Melissa just wouldn't know her time was up.

CHAPTER THREE

Christopher Ross slowly got up from the dirty grimy couch he'd been lying on for the past few hours. He walked unsteadily over to the refrigerator, a cigarette dangling out of the corner of his mouth. The blanket he'd wrapped around him to stave off the cold desert air that seeped in through the cracks of his tarpaper shack dragged along the floor behind him. He couldn't afford to turn on the small electric space heater, because if he did, it would blow the circuit breaker, and he needed the electricity to keep his beer cold.

He opened the refrigerator to take out a beer, but he couldn't find one. He usually made sure he'd still have a couple left before he went to the store for his weekly replenishment of cigarettes and beer, but he'd miscalculated. It was hard to see anything in the refrigerator, because he'd never replaced the bulb when it had burned out several months earlier. He stooped down and searched the shelves again, his hand groping along the back, willing a cold can to magically appear. It was not to be. There was only one thing he could do. He just hoped his truck would start, because he desperately needed to go down the hill to the Quick 'N Go and get more beer, and as long as he was there, more cigarettes.

Ten minutes later, he walked into the store, ignoring the disapproving looks of some customers, as his truck, parked near the entrance of the store, sputtered and expelled black smoke. He had to leave the truck running, because he was afraid he'd never get it started again if he turned off the engine. He didn't bother to tell the customers giving him the evil eye that he couldn't afford to get a smog check. Anyway, the only place he ever went in the truck was the Quick 'N Go to buy his beer, cigarettes, a little food, and cash his monthly check.

He put a carton of cigarettes and two cases of beer on the counter and paid for them. Christopher knew he'd have to make these last, because it would be several more days before he got his next disability check. He picked up the sack the attendant pushed towards him, and as he turned to leave, he saw the Desert Sun newspaper displayed in the news rack. The headline caught his eye.

"Mega Millions Lotto Makes Everything Possible." All he could think about was what he could do with mega millions. As he walked by the rack, he noticed a photo of a woman named Melissa Ross, and paused to take a closer look.

"What the…" he said to himself, setting the sack and beer down and scratching his temple. He squinted at the photo of the woman and thought it looked a lot like his niece, the ungrateful upstart who'd just walked away from his shack one day without even saying goodbye or 'thanks for taking care of me for all these years.' When he'd gotten up from his nap that day to tell her he was ready for her to cook his dinner, she was gone. And the self-centered little brat had never contacted him since.

He knew the chances of the Melissa Ross in the newspaper article being his niece were pretty remote, but he turned back to the cashier and said, "I'll take this paper." He put a dollar bill on the counter, and she carefully counted out his change.

When he was back in his battered old brown truck, he could just make out the newspaper print in the dim late afternoon sunlight. He quickly scanned the article for anything that might indicate that the Melissa Ross in the article was his niece. When Christopher read the sentence, "Ms. Ross said she has to be one of the luckiest people in the world. When she was growing up in an area called Four Corners and living behind a gas station, she never could have imagined how her life would turn out. Now, several years after winning millions, she enjoys a life most people can only dream of." He inhaled sharply and reread the sentence two more times, then headed for his shack, his head spinning with ideas of what he should do with the information.

He hurried to open the screen door on the shack and in doing so, took the part that was still clinging to the rusted hinge completely off of it. He threw it down in disgust, grabbed a beer out of the case he'd just bought, and took the newspaper with him to the dilapidated couch. Christopher read the article several more times, but each time he read it, he became more and more certain that the Melissa Ross in the article was his dead brother's daughter, his niece. The article talked about the odds of winning something like the Mega Millions Lotto and the changes it had made in her life. The woman was quoted as saying she now considered herself to be a philanthropist and an art and antique connoisseur.

"I'll bet she is, the smug thankless brat," Christopher sneered, draining the can of beer and scrunching it in his hand before he tossed it on the floor.

His heart raced as he read how she said her mother had been responsible for teaching her to appreciate the beauty in art and antiques, but she'd never thought she'd be able to afford them. The article went on to say that in the years since she'd won one of the largest payoffs in the history of the Mega Millions Lotto, she had amassed a formidable collection of art and antiques, as well as being referred to as a "doyenne" or "the most respected woman among Palm Springs charitable donors." The article also outlined how she felt a particular need to help children, since she'd had no help when she was growing up. It concluded by saying she felt she had a responsibility to do something good with the money she'd been so fortunate to win.

Become quite the little saint, haven't ya'? Now I wonder what I should do about this turn of events, Christopher thought. *Sounds like she's sitting on a ton of money, and I'm her only living relative. The article had said she had no family. Last I heard, her good-for-nothing snot-nosed brother was doin' time for drug dealin'. The East Side Victoria gang sure didn't do him no good. Man, would I like to get my hands on some of that money. Course she wouldn't have nuthin' to do with the likes of me, now that she's a hoity-toity rich Palm Springs lah-di-dah lady. I'll just have to figure out the best way to get it. Ain't got much else to do and, hey, if she was to die, I'd get it all.*

He got up from the couch and popped open another beer, holding it up in a mock toast. "Jes' like Bob Dylan sang, 'the times they are a-changin', and man am I ready for 'em to. Think my ship finally done got here. Now I jes' got to figure out how to get on board."

CHAPTER FOUR

"Here, let me help you with your cufflinks," Marty said to her husband, Detective Jeff Combs. "After all, it's not every night we get to go to one of the biggest charity events of the year and sit with the chairwoman and her husband. We must be important," she said as she stepped away from him and smiled.

"Number one, I do not want to go to this thing and wear a monkey suit." Jeff winced, and ran a finger around the inside of his dress shirt collar, trying to loosen it. "Number two, I'd be much happier sitting out in our courtyard with Laura, Lee, and John," he said, referring to the other three people who lived in the four-home compound located a few miles outside of Palm Springs in the small community of High Desert.

"And number three, we are definitely not important."

Marty's face fell, just a little.

"No, I shouldn't say that. I am definitely not important," Jeff continued. "You are, just because you're you, but I do want to remind you that the only reason we're going to the Charity for Children's annual gala is because the police chief has out of town guests and needed someone to substitute for him. Unfortunately, that substitute is me. I hate this type of an event. Everyone's trying to outdo everyone else, and I think there must be some unwritten law that states if you attend one of these things, you have to be phonier than the next person.'"

Marty put her lipstick on and said, "Jeff, it won't be that bad. We'll have a good meal, and maybe we can pick something up at the silent auction. After all, there will probably be some pretty fabulous items donated for the auction, given who will be attending the gala. The Desert Sun has been talking it up for weeks as being the, and I quote, 'premiere event of the season.'" She put her hand on her hip and posed with one foot forward, her knee slightly bent. "I know I'm changing the subject, but how do you like my dress?"

He walked over to her and put his arms around her. "Marty, you make anything you wear look good. Believe me when I tell you later tonight that when people are looking at the head table, they won't be looking at me or anyone else. You'll be the focus of their attention, and it's probably a good thing the chief won't be attending this event."

She stepped back and looked up at him. "Why?"

"Because you're going to stop traffic in that dress, which is a misdemeanor in Palm Springs," he said, grinning.

"Thanks for the compliment, I guess," she answered. "I've never worn anything quite like this, but then again, I've never been to an event quite like tonight's either." She walked over to look at herself in the full-length mirror, pleased with the way the long-sleeved peach sheath, with its plunging neckline, hugged her curves and showed them off to their best advantage. The color of the dress was a perfect accompaniment to her hazel eyes and auburn-colored hair which she wore in a soft chignon.

The only jewelry she wore was her wedding ring and diamond stud earrings, a recent gift from herself to herself after she'd completed a large antique appraisal for an East Coast family who wintered in Palm Springs. The three-week appraisal had furnished her with a very large fee, and Jeff was adamant that she use it to do something just for herself.

Jeff looked over at her, "Marty, your eyelid is twitching. Laura told me you only do that when you're nervous, and other than when you said 'I do,' when we got married, I'm not sure I can remember a time when you've ever done that before. What are you nervous about?"

"I am not nervous," she said in a voice that told him that was the end of the conversation. However, her words hung in the air, and a moment later she let out a sigh. "Okay, I admit it. I'm on edge. I've never been to something this prestigious, and I've never sat at a head table before. What if I do something to embarrass you?"

He walked over to her and put his hand under her chin, drawing her eyes up to his. "Marty, trust me. Every man who sees you tonight will be envious of me. You are my biggest asset. Never forget that."

She put her arms around his neck drawing him towards her and lightly brushed her lips against his. "Thanks, Jeff. I really needed that. I'm fine now. Honest."

"Well, if nothing else, your eyelid has stopped twitching, so that's a good sign. We better go now. If I don't do my proper duty here, the chief will probably assign the worst cases that come through the station to me."

Together, they walked outside, followed by Duke, the black Labrador retriever Marty had bought when she'd moved to High Desert following her divorce. Laura, her sister, had insisted she live in one of the homes Laura owned in the four-house compound. Fortunately, Laura worked for an insurance company that specialized in insuring personal property owned by high wealth individuals, and she'd been able to help Marty get clients for her art and antique appraisal business. It had been a huge help to Marty initially, but since then, she'd been able to develop an excellent reputation in the Palm Springs area and now most of her business was through referral from previous clients.

Trailing right behind Duke was the newest addition to Jeff and Marty's household, Patron, a white six-month-old boxer puppy Jeff had given Marty for helping him solve one of his murder investigations. The two dogs had bonded, and whenever you saw Duke, you knew Patron would be right there as well.

As was their usual practice, every evening the residents of the compound gathered in the common courtyard to share the events of their day, have a glass of wine, and taste-test recipes that John, the owner of The Red Pony food truck, prepared for them in exchange for their honest opinions and a little stipend.

Tonight was no exception, and all of them were sitting at the large picnic table where John served them dinner every night. Lee looked up and let out a wolf whistle as Marty and Jeff walked over to the table and sat down. "Marty, you look fabulous, and Jeff, you clean up okay, but if I were you, I wouldn't let her out of my sight tonight!"

"Thanks," Jeff said wryly. "Trust me, I'd much rather be here with all of you than going to some event where I have to wear a monkey suit. This is just not my kind of thing."

"Where are you going?" John asked.

"To the Charity for Children fundraiser gala. I guess it's a pretty big deal, and we're even going to be seated at the head table. My chief had out-of-town guests and suggested, might I say strongly suggested, that it would be in the best interests of my future with the department if I attended it on his behalf."

"I don't envy you," John said with a raised eyebrow. "Max and I recently catered a cocktail party for Tammy Crawford. She's a big society maven and will probably be there tonight. She's a real piece of work. Just try not to sit next to her. She has this thing about being the most prominent philanthropist in the Palm Springs area. We couldn't get her out of the kitchen while we were prepping for the event. All she could talk about was how much she hated, as she put it, that nouveau riche upstart woman, Melissa Ross. Said that real philanthropists came from old money, not upstarts who got their money by picking numbers in a lottery. Her words weren't very charitable, if you ask me."

"I'll keep your words of wisdom in mind, but I'd guess it's already been arranged where everyone will sit, so rather doubt I have a say in the matter," Jeff said.

Laura piped up, her face solemn. "Marty, you do look stunning, but you need to be very aware of everything you see tonight. I don't know why, but I'm getting a very strong message that tonight is going to be a decisive time for what's going to be happening in the next few days."

"Laura, I wish you wouldn't do that," Marty said, turning to her sibling. "We all know you have these psychic abilities, but whenever you say something like that it gives me the heebie-jeebies, and tonight is not a night when I want to experience them. I have enough to cope with already."

She looked sternly at her sister, and knew that if anyone were to meet Laura, they'd never in a million years take her for a psychic. She didn't have a crystal ball, she didn't wear a turban, and she didn't chant things none of them could understand. Even so, the others had learned they better listen when Laura said something like what she'd just said.

"Laura, you know you've made a believer out of me, but can you at least give Marty and me a hint?" Worry was etched across Jeff's face. "This is going to be bad enough as it is. I don't want to have to look over my shoulder and Marty's the entire time we're there without a clue what I'm looking for."

Laura shrugged apologetically. "Jeff, you've been around me long enough to know that when I get a strong feeling like this, I hate to say it, but I'm usually right. I am getting a feeling of feminine energy, if that helps."

"Well, I suppose eliminating half of the people who will be attending tonight is better than nothing," he said laughing. He held his arm out to Marty. "Your chariot is waiting, Cinderella."

"Just one minute." Marty bent over and gave Patron and Duke a goodbye pat. "Be good for Auntie Laura, and we'll be back soon."

They were all taken by surprise when Patron growled. That was the first time the white bundle of fur had ever done that.

"What's up with that growl, Patron?" Marty asked. "This is a first." She turned towards Jeff. "Do you think he's okay?"

"You're probably not going to like what I'm going to say, but I'm getting a very strong vibe that this dog is psychic," Laura said. She looked at the others, each of whom was looking at her in disbelief. "I'm just telling you what I'm being told by whatever. And really, it's not all that unusual. Think about storm-sensing dogs, dogs who can tell when their owner is going to have a bout with epilepsy, or even those who can detect cancer. I don't know what Patron is sensing, but he's definitely channeling something, and it's as if he's warning you, Marty."

"Swell, that's all I need. First a sister who's a psychic and now a dog who's on the same other-worldly wavelength. Jeff, I think we should have left directly and never come out here to say goodbye." Marty stood up with a laugh. "We're off for whatever. Wish us luck. We'll tell you all about it tomorrow."

"Oops, Marty, I almost forgot," Laura said. "Dick called and asked if you could do an appraisal for a woman named Melissa Ross." She looked over at John and said, "It's probably the woman you were just talking about. From what Dick said she won the lottery several years ago and has amassed a huge art and antique collection that needs to be appraised. He thought it would be a good idea if I took both of you to lunch, and you could discuss it with her and set up a time. He'd like to get it started sooner rather than later, so I suggested we meet Monday. I've already checked with Melissa, and she can do it. Okay with you?"

"Sure, shall we go to our favorite Mexican restaurant or is that not fancy enough?"

Laura shook her head. "Not fancy enough. I thought we'd go to

Melvyn's. It's an experience, and I don't think you've been there yet. The restaurant has been around for fifty years, and all the stars like Frank Sinatra used to go. It's known for making dishes like Steak Diane at your tableside. And the waiters - I think all of them have been there since it opened. Anyway, have a good time mingling with all the important people of Palm Springs."

"Yeah, right," Jeff said as he held the gate to the compound open for Marty and at the same time gave Patron the "stay" command, since it was clear the little guy had every intention of accompanying them.

CHAPTER FIVE

"I'm sorry, Ed, but you have a disease called Valley Fever," the prison doctor said. "The results of the chest x-rays and the blood and culture tests all point to one of the worst cases I've seen since we started diagnosing it in 1990. I know you're getting out of prison tomorrow, so I'm sure this is the last thing you want to hear from me."

"Sorry, Doc. Don't have a clue what that is. All I know is I haven't felt good for a couple of months. Seems like I've been coughin' for a long time and figured that's why I was gettin' the headaches and just generally feelin' lousy. How did I get it, and what can I do about it?"

"The disease is primarily caused by a fungus that's in the soil in this part of the San Joaquin Valley as well as other areas of the Southwest. Wish I could be clearer, but that's essentially it. It gets windy here in Delano, and I'd bet you caught it when you were exercising out in the prison yard."

Ed coughed violently and then said in a raspy voice, "That's all well and good, Doc, but now what? Got some special medicine for me to take?"

The doctor looked Ed straight in the eye. "Son, I don't know how to tell you this. The good news is that you're going to be a free man starting tomorrow. The bad news is that there is no known cure for a case of Valley Fever as serious as yours." He turned away, reaching down for his battered black leather doctor's bag.

"Wait a minute. Are you givin' me some kind of a death verdict? Is that what yer' sayin'?" Ed asked as he began to cough again.

"I'm not God, Ed, and miracles happen. All I do is report on what I see. Let's just hope there's a miracle in your future."

Ed was quiet for several long moments and then said, "How long do you think I have?"

"I don't know. As I said a moment ago, miracles happen, but if one doesn't, I'd say about six months or so. I'll give you some cough medicine now. I'm also going to start you on a new medicine, Noxafil. I'll give you a prescription for both when you leave here. Valley Fever is a relatively new disease and quite frankly, there have been very few cases as serious as yours. It's not curable, but we can try to make what time you've got left comfortable. I really am sorry to be the bearer of such bad news."

The doctor looked at his watch and said, "I have to go, but your medicine should be here within the hour. Hopefully, that will give you some relief from your cough. Good luck." Leaving Ed's bedside, he hurriedly walked over to the steel door of the cramped cell before pausing and turning back towards Ed. "Since you're getting out of here soon, you might want to start a list of the things you want to do. My advice is don't waste any time, Ed. Do them."

He rapped on the door, and the prison guard standing on the other side of the cell door let him out.

Swell, Ed thought. *Have a nice day and by the way, ya' ain't got long to live, so do what's on your bucket list. Sheesh, I've been in the joint for twenty-five years, so yeah, there's a lot I want to do. Took the fall for the brothers and sure never heard no more from them, other than a couple of 'em that were baby gangsters with me and ended up in here. People dis the gang members, but man, they covered my back more than once. Nice to have someone watchin' yer' back when yer' in prison.*

The door slid open again, and a nurse entered. "Mr. Ross, I've brought you some medication and some newspapers. Thought you might like a change from having nothing to do but watch television. First, take this capsule and the cough medicine for me." The nurse waited while he swallowed the pill with the water she'd given him and then carefully measured out a spoonful of cough medicine. "Very good. Now, here are the newspapers. I brought you the Los Angeles Times and the Desert Sun. Since you'll be leaving here tomorrow, might as well go to Palm Springs and see what the wealthy folks down there are doing these days."

After the nurse left, Ed felt tired and soon fell asleep. The cough medicine was formulated to ease the severity of coughing, but those same ingredients caused patients to sleep. Three hours later he awoke with a strange feeling that something was wrong. Then he remembered his conversation with the doctor. He was going to die in a few months. He was finally getting out of prison, but he'd soon be a dead man. Talk about irony. So much for the old gang members talk of him working in the new gang.

Ed was only forty-three years old. It never occurred to him that he'd die at such a young age. He had things he wanted to do. He wanted some nice wheels. He remembered the 1955 black and white Chevrolet convertible Spider had owned. He'd tricked it out, and it was one bad car. Ed wanted one just like it. And clothes. He'd worn nothing but an orange prison jumpsuit for the last twenty-five years. He deserved some nice threads.

And where does someone who has no job or money and is near death go? he wondered. *Maybe to a county hospital. The prison hospital can't take me in because I won't be a State of California prisoner.*

Suddenly, leaving prison was a scary thought. He had no money and no place to go, and he was running out of time. At least if he were to live out his last days in prison, he'd be looked after by nurses who treated him with respect, and he wouldn't have any medical bills to pay.

His head hurt from all the thinking he was doing, so he decided to read the newspapers the nurse had brought him. He read the Los Angeles Times and thought not much had changed while he'd been in prison. People were still getting killed, politicians were still being caught in scandals, and whatever the celebrities did was still worth being written about. He picked up the Desert Sun, figuring there was nothing in there that would be of interest to a kid who came from the outskirts of Barstow and was a soon to be an ex-con. He was leafing from one page to another when a name leapt off a page at him. Melissa Ross.

That was the name displayed under a photograph of a woman on the society page of the paper. It had been his sister's name, but he figured she'd gotten married, and he'd never see her again. She sure had never tried to find him. He read the article twice. It was about how she'd donated three million dollars to the Children for Charity event in Palm Springs which had been held the previous evening.

It made mention of the fact that she was considered to be the leading philanthropist in the Palm Springs area and even had a quote from her. "One of the best days in my life was when I compared the numbers on my lottery ticket to the winning Mega Millions drawing numbers and they matched. There will never be another feeling quite like that."

The article went on to state that her windfall had allowed her to indulge in two things she'd wanted to do since she was a child – give money to charitable causes she considered to be important and surround herself with beautiful art and antiques. The article concluded by saying she was looking forward to the upcoming antiques and fine arts auction that was going to be held in Palm Springs, since it was the first time a really large auction house had held such an event in the city.

Ed spent a long time studying the photograph of the woman shown in the paper. He hadn't seen his sister for a long, long time, but he thought there was a resemblance to the young woman he'd known. He didn't know much about plastic surgery, but it looked like her nose was a little straighter. He remembered that she'd had a bump on it from when she'd fallen off the gas station roof. He smiled involuntarily, remembering how they used to get on the roof and play. Four Corners definitely wasn't a child-friendly place to grow up in.

The smile turned to a frown as he realized his sister was now a very wealthy woman, and not only did he have nothing, he was going to die broke and in pain. It wasn't fair. He wondered if she'd give him some of her money if he told her he was terminally ill. He thought about it for a few minutes, but he decided that was probably a dead-end street, considering how she'd always lectured him about being in a gang and that no good would come of it. He even remembered how she'd once said, "Mark my words. You'll end up in prison or worse, and if you don't get out of the gang, I want nothing more to do with you." He'd left the tarpaper shack a few days later and never returned.

Ed didn't think Melissa would be amenable to a deathbed reconciliation with her long-lost brother. The more he thought about it, the madder he got. He was sick and was going to die on loser street. Meanwhile, his prissy sister had everything. Money, a glamorous lifestyle, and she was so rich she could afford to give three million bucks to some charity he'd never heard of. She'd had her share of the good life, now it was his turn.

He really didn't have much to lose by committing murder, and he was pretty sure she'd agree to see him, maybe when she was on a high after attending the auction described in the paper. There had been a lengthy article in the paper about it which he hadn't paid much attention to.

Ed picked up the paper again and this time, carefully noted all the details about the auction. He put it down and thought about the gate money he'd be given when he got out of prison. Two hundred dollars. Big deal. They should have instructions on it like "Don't spend it all at once." It was a pittance for the time he'd served, but he thought it would be enough for him to get a bus ride to Palm Springs and find a cheap motel. He had no idea if his uncle was still alive, but other than him, Ed was her only living relative, and he was closer in kin to her than their uncle He thought even if his uncle was alive, it was unlikely he knew anything about Melissa. The article in the paper had stated that she was free to do as she wished with her money, because she was the last surviving member of her family.

He didn't think she'd greet him with open arms, but all he needed was for her to open the front door to her home. He'd handle it from there.

CHAPTER SIX

Thirty minutes after they'd left the compound, Marty and Jeff entered the La Quinta Resort, one of the premier hotel and golf courses in the Palm Springs area, and certainly one of the oldest.

"Jeff, this is beautiful. I've heard of this hotel ever since I moved to High Desert, but I've never seen it. I mean look at this dramatic entry." They were driving along a divided brick road with a center median filled with flowers, palm trees, and Italian cypress trees. In the twilight, Marty could just make out the mountains that backed up to the resort. She gasped in delight. "Look at all of those beautiful fountains that are scattered everywhere around the resort property. I don't know why I was dreading tonight. It's just gorgeous. No wonder the gala is being held here."

Jeff smiled, turned onto the curved driveway, and stopped in front of a line of waiting valets. "Welcome to the La Quinta Resort," the uniformed valet said as he held the door open for Marty. Jeff gave his car keys to the valet and then took Marty's elbow as they walked into the large lobby. A sign directed them to the Charity for Children event and they began to walk down a long hall. They weren't the only ones attending the gala, judging from the large number of tuxedo-clad men and elegantly dressed women in the hallway.

Two long tables, one on either side of the double doors leading to the grand ballroom where the gala was being held, served as sign-in tables. One had the letters "A-M" attached to the wall behind it, and the other had the letters "N-Z" behind it. Jeff steered Marty over to the first table and said, "Mr. and Mrs. Combs." He smiled at Marty and said, "I know professionally you go by Marty Morgan, but it makes me feel good to say Mrs. Combs."

"Me, too," she said smiling back at him, reaching out to hold his hand. "We should have date nights more often."

The young woman sitting at the table was properly attired for the gala in a nondescript simple black dress. From the lack of important jewelry and the way she was dressed, Marty was pretty sure she was an employee of the nonprofit organization, rather than one of the committee or board members. She handed Jeff and Marty a card that contained their auction bidding number and table number, which was number one.

"Let's go into the auction room, get a glass of wine, and see if there's anything there we can't live without," Jeff said, nodding towards the room across the hall. They entered the room which contained about everything that would appeal to anyone who wanted to take something home in exchange for donating money to a charitable cause. Waiters carried trays with various types of canapes which she and Jeff tried out in the hopes of being able to find something that they could share with John so he could serve it at one of the many different events he catered.

Jeff told the waiter he didn't want to spoil his dinner by eating anything else, but Marty took the napkin the waiter handed her along with two different appetizers. A moment later, she turned to Jeff and said, "The waiter's over there. You have to get one. I can't tell you how good these are, and I need your help in describing them to John. These would be perfect for him to serve."

Jeff walked over to the waiter and helped himself to the two appetizers Marty was raving about. When he returned, he took a bite and said, "Agreed. These are absolutely wonderful. I've had stuffed mushrooms before, but never one as good as this one. Why don't you go talk to the waiter and see if he knows what's in them? I'm sure

John could recreate it."

"I will, and I also want to ask him about the shrimp and grits puff pastry. That is really different. Back in a minute."

She walked over to the waiter and when Jeff saw Marty take a pen and a small paper pad out of her cocktail purse, he was pretty sure she'd gotten the ingredients, if not the full recipes, for the two appetizers.

"Mission accomplished," she said when she returned a few minutes later. "I got the recipes, and after I type them up, I'll give them to John. Of course, I'll have to request that he make them for all of us so Laura and Lee can try them as well. In my opinion, the evening is already a success."

"I'm sure John would agree with you," Jeff said.

An hour later they heard a bell ring indicating that dinner was ready to be served as well as blinking lights in the room emphasizing it. At the same time a voice came over the microphone advising that the silent auction would be ending in five minutes. Frantic guests rushed to put their last bids on the items they wanted.

When Marty and Jeff entered the banquet room the first thing they noticed was bouquets of exotic flowers everywhere – from the centerpieces to the large standing vases on the stage and scattered around the perimeter of the room. The brightly colored orange and blue birds of paradise, soft yellow and white plumerias, various colors of purple orchids, pink and red heliconias, and yellow hibiscus plants, all matched with various kinds of greenery was simply breath-taking.

"Jeff, I've never seen most of these flowers, but they're simply gorgeous," Marty said, her eyes widening.

"I recall from the invitation the chief gave me, that the theme of tonight's gala is 'Tropical Paradise.' All those flowers look a whole lot different than what I saw when I was growing up in the Midwest. I agree, they really are beautiful. Ah, here's our table, directly in front of the center of the stage. I see a woman who I assume is our hostess showing people where to sit. Smile, we're up next."

He placed his hand in the small of Marty's back and they walked up to the woman. "By any chance would you be Tammy Crawford?" he asked her.

"I certainly am, and since I know everyone else sitting at the table, I assume that you're Detective Combs and this must be your wife, Marty. Welcome to the annual gala for Charity for Children. I'm sorry the chief couldn't make it, but I'm glad you were able to fill in for him. Marty, why don't you sit next to me, and your husband can sit on the other side of you."

As they were getting seated Tammy introduced them to the others at the table and said, "Last, but certainly not least, I'd like to introduce you to my husband, Lew Crawford. I'm sure you've heard of him. He's in the papers almost every week with news about his business, Crawford Investments. It's the largest hedge fund headquartered on the West Coast" she said smugly. "He's so generous with me, and because of it, I've become the number one philanthropist in Palm Springs."

"Glad you could join us," Lew said, "but I think Tammy's days as the largest charitable donor may be coming to an end. As they say in the movies, there's a new kid on the block, Melissa Ross."

"Don't be silly," Tammy said, her face reddening. "That upstart nothing, who got all her money by a fluke, will never surpass me. It's ridiculous to even consider it. Nouveau riche people always try to buy their way into society. She'll never be accepted in this town."

"Hate to disappoint you, darling, but think your time as the number one philanthropist is up," Lew said as he picked up his drink. "I just heard that she made an extremely large contribution to the Charity for Children this afternoon. One that's going to make you look like a second-string player."

"You must be kidding! That woman has no right to do something like that. I will not give up my place as the number one philanthropist to that piece of Barstow trash." Tammy was speaking in a low voice with a bright smile on her face. No one who was observing her from afar would ever think the chairwoman of the gala was anything other than pleased with the way the evening was panning out.

She was interrupted by a young woman who walked over to the table and said, "Excuse me, but I have the pleasure of giving this winning bid card to Detective Combs." She looked around and saw Jeff gesturing to her, his forehead creased.

"Pardon me, Miss, but I think there's been a misunderstanding. I don't believe I bid on anything."

Marty interrupted him. "I'm Mrs. Combs, and I'm the one who bid." She looked over at Jeff with an innocent expression on her face. "Well, you left to get us a glass of wine, so I thought I'd bid on something. I guess I won." The silent auction worker handed her a card and a credit card machine. Marty opened her purse, withdrew her credit card, inserted it in the machine, and signed the charge ticket. "Thank you very much."

"No, it's we who thank you for your generous contribution to a worthwhile cause." The worker smiled and handed Marty back her credit card. "You can pick up your purchase on the way out. If anyone questions you, just show them your bid card. I signed it, showing that it's been paid in full."

As soon as she'd left, Jeff leaned closer to Marty and said, "Mind telling me what we, and you notice I'm accentuating the word we, bought at the silent auction?"

"Uhh, I really think we should support such a worthy cause, don't you?" she asked with a beguiling smile.

"I'm getting the distinct impression that whatever you bought is something I probably would not have. Would I be right?"

"Okay, you're going to find out anyway. I bought rhinestone

studded dog collars for Duke and Patron. Duke's is red, and Patron's is black." Marty sat back and waited for his reaction which wasn't long in coming.

At that moment a waiter served their salads, giving Jeff a little time to compose himself. When he finally spoke, he said in a very soft voice, "Marty, I'm trying not to judge you, and you know I'm fine with whatever you want to buy, but I've got to tell you the dogs will never wear rhinestone collars. What were you thinking? These are male dogs that live in the desert, for Pete's sake. They're not pampered Hollywood pooches."

"That may be true," she said defensively, "but they don't get many treats, and I thought they'd look good in them."

"I beg to differ with you about them never getting any treats. Have you ever noticed how every night after dinner they follow John and Max back to John's kitchen? I don't think they're doing that for a pat on the head. I'd be more inclined to think it was for food treats, wouldn't you?"

Maty smiled sheepishly. "Well, yes, now that you mention it."

Their conversation was interrupted by Tammy. "So tell me, Marty, what does a detective's wife do when her husband is busy catching bad guys?"

Marty thought it would be prudent not to mention that she often helped Jeff catch the bad guys, but she chose to simply tell Tammy about her art and antique appraisal business.

They continued to talk through dinner, although their conversation was interrupted from time to time by people congratulating Tammy on being the chairwoman of another successful event. Several times Marty heard her say, "Well, you do know my passion is philanthropy."

No question her ego is definitely fed by her role as a philanthropist. I think that's the first time I've ever met anyone who defined themselves that way.

Interesting, Marty thought.

After the waiters had cleared the entrees from the tables, the Executive Director of the Charity for Children walked up to the podium and tapped the microphone a couple of times to get the audience's attention before speaking into it. "Ladies and gentlemen, may I please have your attention?"

When the room became quiet he began to speak. "My name is Dr. Gordon Jamison, and I am the Executive Director of the Charity for Children. My speech tonight will be short, because the band we hired has to leave promptly at 11:00 p.m. in order to catch a plane for Chicago where they are performing at an early morning breakfast. Believe me, we were very lucky they agreed to honor this commitment, and since we've had them before and they were requested by so many of you, I promised them that if they agreed to perform, I would keep my speech very short.

"I only have two subjects to address, and then the music can begin. The first is to thank each and every one of you for coming tonight and supporting Charity for Children. Because of you, we have raised over two million dollars tonight, and that substantially exceeds what we have raised at previous galas."

He stopped speaking and acknowledged the thunderous applause by joining in the hand clapping that was taking place throughout the room. "Please, please, I am just as happy about it as you are, but remember my promise to the band. I have one more thing to say, and then the band will begin to play."

The crowd quieted and when everyone had stopped clapping, Dr. Jamison said, "What I am about to share with you happened only a few hours ago, so even the wonderful committee who did such a fabulous job in planning and overseeing tonight's event hasn't been told. It is my distinct pleasure to recognize the donor of three million dollars to the Charity for Children, Miss Melissa Ross. Miss Ross, please stand, so we can give you the thanks your generous gift merits."

An attractive woman who appeared to be in her early forties stood up and acknowledged the applause and shouts of bravo with a wave. She wore a broad smile and sat down as the applause abated.

"Miss Ross, on behalf of the Charity for Children, I thank you," Dr. Jamison continued, "While we only met several hours ago, your name is synonymous with good causes, and I'm sure no one would begrudge you the name of Queen of Palm Springs Philanthropy. And while I and the members of this wonderful organization are most grateful for your generosity, it is the children who will benefit in so many ways from this selfless gift of yours."

Again, there was applause. "And Miss Ross, I think it's no secret to anyone who reads the Desert Sun, that with your affinity for art and antiques, this money certainly could have been spent by you on one treasure or another, particularly at the upcoming art and antique auction that's scheduled to take place this coming Tuesday evening. Thanks for putting the children of this region before your passion for beautiful things. Ladies and gentlemen, as I said earlier, my speech would be short, and so it was. Please enjoy the rest of the evening."

Marty noticed that Tammy's husband had put his hand on her arm as if to restrain her, and she saw him whisper something to her. Marty couldn't help but overhear her response.

"I hate that woman," Tammy said bitterly, her voice seething with anger. "I don't know how or what, but I have to do something to stop her. She's just trailer trash, and I hope she remembers this night, because this is the last time she will ever be acknowledged for anything. No one does that to me and gets away with it."

"Keep your voice down and act like you're happy about this," her husband said in a low voice. "People are looking at you, and you know how they talk in this town. You don't want to be a headline tomorrow about a power struggle in the Charity for Children nonprofit organization. This is your night, not hers, no matter how angry you are, don't let it show."

Marty didn't acknowledge that she'd overheard them and

pretended to listen to what the woman on the other side of Jeff was saying about the different ways that the charity helped children. Waiters began the dessert service and the band started playing. In a few moments Marty noticed that Tammy and her husband had walked over to the table where Melissa Ross was sitting and she watched as the two women hugged in a public show of amity. Marty began to wonder if what she'd heard Tammy say to her husband was a figment of her imagination.

She made a mental note to tell Jeff what had occurred on the way home. She took a bite of the dessert and couldn't figure out if it was a brownie or a piece of cake, but whatever it was, John deserved to know about it.

"Jeff, how do you like this dessert?" she asked.

"I think it's fabulous, but I can't figure out what it is or what's in it. Is it something we should tell John about?"

"Definitely. I have to go to the ladies' room. On the way, I'll stop and ask one of the waiters what it is, but whatever it is, it's really, really good. Back in a minute. Don't get into any trouble while I'm gone," she said as she stood up.

"In this crowd?" Jeff asked. "Not a chance."

A few minutes later Marty returned and sat down, noticing that all of their tablemates were on the dance floor. "Jeff, the waiter said it's called a Jack and Coke cake. He said the Jack is from a small amount of Jack Daniels whiskey in it and the Coke, is just that, Coca Cola. Weird ingredients. He said he didn't have the recipe, and the hotel chef never gives out his recipes, but he confided that he'd taken a piece of the cake, as he called it, home one night and his wife had found a recipe for it on the internet. He suggested I try that. I'll tell John about it tomorrow."

"Sounds like a good idea to me. Marty, you know how much I hate to dance. I feel like I'm back in junior high school. I just hate it. Why don't we quietly leave while everyone is out on the dance floor?"

"Fine by me, but don't you think we should thank our hostess?"

Jeff stood up and pulled out Marty's chair. "I'll drop her a note tomorrow on official stationery. She'd probably like to show it off or put it up on her wall. She can't do that if I just thank her."

"Good point, plus if we leave now we'll beat the crowd at the valet stand. If we leave when everyone else does, we'll be standing in line for hours."

"Couldn't agree more. Come on, we're out of here."

CHAPTER SEVEN

"Isabella, you're late. I've been waiting a long time for you to get home and cook my dinner," the handsome Hispanic man said as he put down the glass he'd been drinking from. "Where have you been?"

"I stopped by the church to see Father O'Malley after I left Miss Ross' house. I wanted to tell him the good news," the soft-spoken small dark-haired woman said. "I know I promised you that I wouldn't tell anyone we were getting married quite yet, but since he will be the one marrying us, I felt he should know." She walked over to where he was sitting at the kitchen table, a bottle of tequila in front of him.

"Tomas, I thought you promised me you wouldn't drink this anymore. You know what it does to you. Please, let me put it away." Isabella said as she picked up the half-empty bottle and walked over to the cabinet where it was kept.

"*Mi amor*, I was worried about you and you know it helps me when I get anxious or I'm concerned about something. I was thinking about how we are going to live when we're married. You're lucky. You were born here so you're a citizen, but me, that's another story. I can't get a job without a green card, and there is no way I can get citizenship papers. I refuse to work as a gardener or out in the fields, so that means we'll have no money when we get married."

"Maybe Father O'Malley could help you get a job. He knows a lot of people in town. I'm sure he could help us."

"Isabella, he's a nice man, but he's not a miracle worker. Anyway, I've been thinking, and I've come up with a plan."

"You always come up with strange, off-the-wall plans when you drink tequila. Remember, you promised me you would stop when we get married. You will, won't you?" she asked in a tentative voice. "I don't like to be around you when you drink too much. Remember what happened that one time."

"How could I forget because you constantly remind me of it? I didn't mean to hit you. It just happened. Matter of fact, it could have happened to anyone. My hand slipped. Now, about my plan," he said in a dismissive tone of voice. "Sit down, because you're involved."

"Are you going to go back to school?" she asked hopefully, as she sat down at the table as he had told her to do.

"No, school's for people who can't think of any other way to make money. I've come up with a foolproof way to make money. Miss Ross has a lot of art and antiques, and you know pretty much where they came from, don't you?" Tomas asked.

"Yes," she answered hesitantly, not liking the way this conversation was going.

"Good. That's what I'm planning on. If something bad were to happen to Miss Ross, then someone could get into her house and take a lot of her expensive things away. Those things could be on their way to some big auction house in Los Angeles by the time anyone got around to figuring out if anything was missing. Get me some more tequila, Isabella. Talking about this makes me thirsty."

Isabella reluctantly walked over to the cabinet, reached up, and retrieved the bottle. She walked back to the table, sat down in front of him and said, "Tomas, I don't like what you're saying."

"I don't care whether you like it or not. I've thought about what we will do for money when we're married, and I can't think of anything else. That is, if you still want to get married," he said as he poured the clear liquid from the bottle and filled his glass to the brim.

"Oh, Tomas, you know there is nothing I want more than to be your wife. We will be so happy together. What is your plan?"

"I read in the paper that Miss Ross is going to attend the art auction that is going to be held here in town on Tuesday night. The article said it will be the largest auction ever held in Palm Springs with very fine artwork and antiques being put up for sale. You know she'll buy heavily. She'll probably even have a few drinks at the auction or afterwards.

"When she gets home from the auction, her driver will let her out at the front door of her house. If she buys some items at the auction, he'll probably help her carry them inside. Once he's gone and she's put her auction purchases away, I'm sure she will head for bed. Once she goes to her bedroom, you can call me. I'll be in my truck parked a few blocks down the street. You can let me in through the kitchen door, and don't worry, if Miss Ross hears us, I'll take care of her. You know how remote that street she lives on is, so no one will see me or my truck. I'll load up the truck and take off for Los Angeles. I know a guy there who takes things from rich people and sells them to some antique shops that don't look too closely at where they came from."

He sat back and took a long drink from his glass of tequila.

"Tomas, you said 'I'll load up the truck and take off for Los Angeles,' but what about me?" Isabella asked, her small hands clasped tightly together.

"You will leave the house with me when I'm through taking out what I can sell. I'll drop you off at our apartment before I leave for Los Angeles. The next day, you'll go into work as if nothing has happened. When Miss Ross discovers that some of her things have been stolen, she'll probably call the cops. You'll have to deal with the police, but don't worry, no one would suspect you. After all, you've been a trusted and loyal employee of Miss Ross for quite a few years. Why would either of us be considered as suspects? Trust me, Isabella, it's a perfect plan."

"She's been very good to me, Tomas. I can't be a part of this. It's wrong. Father O'Malley would say it is a sin. I don't want to live the rest of my life lying in the confessional booth."

"Well," Thomas snarled, as he gulped down the last of the tequila and slammed the empty glass down on the table. "You've got two choices. One is marriage, and the other is no marriage, because if you don't agree to my plan we're not getting married." He stood up, took two steps towards her, and violently pulled her out of her chair by her hair.

"I would hate to have to hurt you again," he said in a soft yet menacing tone, "but if you don't agree to help me with this, I may have to. And we won't be able to get married, because we'll never have enough money. What's your answer, Isabella?"

He yanked her head back and forced her to look at him. "I asked you what your answer is, Isabella. Marriage or no marriage?"

"*Si,* Tomas, *si,*" she said as tears slid down her coffee-colored cheeks.

He released her and sat down again. "Sit, Isabella, we need to make plans."

And I need to decide how I'm going to kill this rich woman if she discovers us in the act of stealing her art and antiques, Tomas thought. *Should be easy enough. I've done it before, only Isabella doesn't know anything about that.*

CHAPTER EIGHT

The following morning, Jeff walked out to the front of the compound and picked up the Desert Sun and the Los Angeles Times from the driveway. When he was walking back to his house, he heard John's voice from across the central courtyard.

"Jeff, I'm making brunch this morning. Mimosas, bagels, and smoked salmon with the works. Plan on 11:00."

"We'll be there. Thanks, John."

He and Marty spent the next two hours reading the paper and trying to work the Sunday crossword puzzle. "Just once I want to finish one," Marty said in frustration as she finally threw her pencil down. "I give up. Time to shower and get ready for brunch."

At 11:00 they walked out the door and over to the long table where Lee, Laura, John, and his associate in the food truck business, Max, were already seated. "Here you go. I squeezed the orange juice just a few minutes ago. It doesn't get much fresher than that," John said as he took two glass mugs from the tray on the table and handed one to each of them.

"Cheers, and how are the High Desert socialites this morning? You don't look any worse for the wear after all your hobnobbing with the rich and famous. Was the party good? More importantly, did you pick up any food ideas for me?"

"That's a lot of questions," Jeff said, taking a sip of his drink. "As a matter of fact, we survived, and Marty was able to get you two appetizer ideas and one dessert, right, Marty?"

"Sure did. After brunch I'll give you my notes. I think you should be able to recreate all three without much trouble, and as a taster, I can tell you that your catering clients will love you for these."

John beamed. "Thanks, I appreciate it. I'm always looking for new dishes, but seriously, how was the gala?"

"It was interesting." Marty turned to her husband. "Jeff, we were so tired when we got home I never did get around to telling you what happened with the chairwoman." She told the group about the auction, and how Jeff had given the cashier the two rhinestone dog collars she'd bought, telling her that he'd decided to donate them for next year's auction.

"Jeff, I couldn't agree more with you about the collars. If Patron and Duke were my dogs, there is no way they'd be wearing sissy rhinestone collars. Marty, what were you thinking?" Lee asked.

"I think I kind of got caught up in the moment," she answered sheepishly. "Anyway, back to the chairwoman, Tammy Crawford. She and Melissa Ross..."

Marty was interrupted by Patron's growling. "What's wrong, little guy?" she asked, reaching her hand out and petting him.

"Something's bothering him about one of the names you just mentioned," Laura said.

Jeff and Marty looked at her in astonishment. "What are you talking about?" Jeff asked. "He's never heard either one of their names."

"Doesn't make any difference. He knows something, and it's not good." Laura looked directly at Marty. "Sorry, Sis, I told you last night that this dog is psychic."

"You've been right about so many things, I almost always trust your judgement, but I do have to say I think you're wrong on this one. I'm sure he's just growling to get attention," Marty said as she continued to pet him.

"Time will tell," Laura said cryptically.

"Anyway, back to the chairwoman," Laura said. "She was not happy about the donation made by Melissa Ross." She went on to tell them about Tammy, her husband, and the large donation.

"Small world," Laura said. "I think I told you the name of the woman we're having lunch with tomorrow. Her name is Melissa Ross. Can't imagine there would be two women in Palm Springs with that name who won the Mega Millions. Should be interesting. Love it when the rich get into catfights."

"I wouldn't exactly call their exchange a catfight, but the chairwoman, and out of deference to Patron, I won't use her name, seemed to be very angry that her title as the number one philanthropist in Palm Springs was being challenged. Evidently it's quite important to her."

"Doesn't particularly surprise me," John said. "Remember, Max and I did a cocktail party for her and that was how she described herself. It's probably pretty upsetting to think the persona you've created is starting to tumble down. If she wasn't so phony, I'd probably feel sorry for her."

"Be that as it may, it really doesn't have anything to do with the appraisal I'll be doing for the other woman whose name I can't mention, other than I overheard what I did and saw their interchange. From what I hear, I already like this woman, and I'm looking forward to meeting her."

*****

"Marty, I'd like to introduce you to Melissa Ross. Melissa, this is the appraiser our company uses, Marty Morgan. She's very, very good, but in full disclosure, she is my sister," Laura said laughing. "I see the hostess is ready to seat us. Melissa, Marty, after you."

A few minutes later after they'd given their orders to the waiter, Marty turned to Melissa and said, "Please tell me about your art and antique collections. I was at the Charity for Children event Saturday night, and I want to tell you how wonderful I think it is that in addition to your art and antiques, you're supporting worthwhile causes like that one. I gathered from what was said about you, your life would make a good story."

Marty never suspected when she said those words just how prophetic they would turn out to be.

Melissa smiled and said, "Yes, my life would probably make a good book or a good movie, but I'm not interested in doing anything in that direction. You may have read that I grew up in Four Corners, which is literally a crossroads for the 395 and 58 highways. We were dirt poor. My father owned a gas station, and we lived in a couple of rooms behind it."

"It's a long jump from being dirt poor to gifting millions to a charity," Laura said as she picked up her water glass.

Marty was looking at Laura as she spoke and noticed that Laura had become uncommonly pale, and her hand was trembling slightly as she picked up her glass. She made a mental note to ask Laura what had caused it. Her eyes were open much wider than usual, as well.

"Yes," Melissa said, looking at Marty and Laura in turn, her eyes masked with sadness. "The poverty and knowing that she was never going to be able to do the things she wanted to do, help people and surround herself with beautiful things, were what caused my mother to commit suicide when I was twelve years old. My father died of a broken heart shortly thereafter. My uncle took my brother and me in, and we lived in a tarpaper shack on the outskirts of Barstow."

Melissa paused. Despite her coiffed silky highlighted hair, manicured nails, and perfectly made up face with sculpted brows, all Marty saw was the pain behind the outwardly carefree mask that Melissa had created for herself.

"Those are years I try not to think too much about," Melissa continued. "My brother became a gang member. I don't know if he's in prison or dead, and I guess I don't care. We all have a choice of whether to do good or bad, and I didn't care for the road he took. So many times, I've thought how it would have hurt my parents if they knew what had become of their son, so maybe it's a good thing they didn't live to see it. I left my uncle, who was a worthless alcoholic, when I'd saved enough money from my job as a waitress. I'd lied about my age to get the job."

"You might want to rethink it. It sounds like it would make a very good movie," Marty said.

"I suppose, but I think there are a lot of other girls who left their homes because of an untenable situation, and mine was just one more. I grew to hate my uncle and fear him. One of the happiest days of my life was when I got on the bus to Palm Springs. I had no idea how I was going to support myself, but I knew whatever it was, it would be better than what I'd had."

"To look at you now, no one would ever guess that was your background," Laura said, her hand still trembling slightly.

"Probably not." The earlier veil of sorrow had lifted from Melissa's blue eyes. "I worked as a waitress in Palm Springs and the only thing that kept me going was the word my mother used to say so often. It became my mantra. The word was 'someday.' I had faith that someday my life would change for the better, and it did. I had very little money, but I scrimped and saved each week so I could buy a ticket for the Tuesday and Friday Mega Millions Lotto drawings.

"And my someday came when I won millions. I've never looked

back. I'm sure a psychiatrist would say the reason I buy art and antiques and give to charities is because I'm trying to recreate a relationship with my mother, and who knows? That might be the reason, but I really don't care. It's what makes me happy, and I can well afford to do it."

"I couldn't agree more. It's kind of like a modern-day fairy tale," Marty said. "Why don't you tell me about your art and antiques? What types do you collect?"

"Growing up in desert areas, I tend to buy paintings that depict desert scenes. I've lived in California my whole life, in fact, I've never been out of the state, even though I could easily afford to travel wherever I want to go. I guess that's why I kind of gravitate towards artwork and antiques that are either representative of California or the Southwest. I also have collected a number of Native American artifacts, probably because I can acquire those rather easily in the antique shops here in Palm Springs."

"Do you specialize in the artwork of any particular artists?"

"Not consciously. I'm kind of one of those people who buys what they like, but I do have several paintings by Edgar Payne, William Wendt, and Granville Redmond. As a matter of fact, I just bought a superb painting by Redmond last week. It's being delivered today. It was kind of a last-minute addition to an auction, but I have a wonderful art consultant who keeps me on top of things like that."

"It's one of my favorite genres as well," Marty said. "Anything else I should be aware of before I come to your home for the appraisal?"

Melissa thought for a moment or two. "I have a pretty extensive Catalina pottery collection as well as a number of pieces by Beatrice Wood. As far as furniture, I tend to collect Mission style furniture. As I'm sure you know, the first Mission piece was a chair designed in 1894 for San Francisco's Swedenborgian Church. After that a manufacturer started making that style of furniture in New York, even though it's loosely based on the missions in California. I like the sleekness and simplicity of it."

"You're very knowledgeable." Marty sensed Melissa wasn't someone who bought blindly based solely on a certain genre or an artist's name. "Do you study the things that are being offered at auction before you buy?"

"Of course. I'd be a fool to bid on something without knowing anything about it. I also have a pretty extensive collection of sterling silver that was made here in California, even some belt buckles."

"I'm really looking forward to seeing all that you have. It's not often that I get to do an appraisal when an owner is as knowledgeable as you are."

"Thank you. Even though I was just a child, I sat with my mother for hours reading magazines about art and antiques. Every week she'd take me to the Barstow library and she'd check out the maximum number of books she could borrow, all of them dealing with art and antiques. I always went with her. When we got home, we'd spend hours looking at them. There wasn't much else to do in Kramer Junction, or as I call it, Four Corners. It was pretty much made up of my dad's gas station and a fast food hamburger stop in the road place," she said laughing ruefully.

"As far as the appraisal," Melissa continued, "why don't you start Wednesday morning about 9:00? There's an auction I'll be attending in Palm Springs tomorrow night, so if I buy anything that doesn't require a delivery, you can do that as well." She looked at her watch. "I'd love to stay and have dessert, but I'm the chairwoman of Stamp Out Homelessness in Palm Springs, and I have an important meeting of that organization I have to attend. I don't know if you're aware of it, but the problem has gotten much worse, and a number of the homeless people are drug addicts, which means they need money to support their habit. Panhandling and petty thefts are becoming the norm in this area. I don't know how much we can do about the problem, but this group is committed to helping that population."

"As a matter of fact, I do know something about it," Marty said with a nod. "My husband is a detective with the Palm Springs Police Department, and he's told me several times that the number of homeless people has risen sharply in the recent past as well as about the drug addiction problem. He also told me he thinks people are drawn here because of the warm climate. Seems to be a lot more attractive to them than the Northern or Midwestern parts of the United States."

"Well, I have no idea where this will go, but as I told you, we're committed to trying to help the homeless," Melissa said as she reached for her purse before getting up to leave. "Laura, good seeing you, and Marty, I'll see you Wednesday morning. My maid, Isabella, will be there if I'm not home for any reason. She can show you where everything is."

"I'm looking forward to it," Marty said. "Seeing beautiful things is definitely one of the advantages of working in my profession."

They both watched Melissa as she said goodbye to the staff of Melvyn's on her way out. From the way she used each of their names, it was obvious she was a regular at the restaurant.

Marty turned back to Laura as she picked up her cup of coffee. "Want to tell me what's going on? You didn't say a word all through lunch."

"What do you mean?" Laura asked.

"Don't give me that. When Melissa was seated and you introduced me to her, you got pale as a ghost and your hand was shaking. You've been trembling ever since. What's that all about? Are you sick?"

"I would have told you sooner or later, but I'm just trying to figure out what's going on. You know, all my life I've had this ability to kind of know things in advance before they happen. I've certainly given you enough advice over the years, and I've never known where those things came from. They just did."

Laura took a sip of her coffee, sighed deeply, and continued, "When Patron came to the compound, I know it sounds silly, but it's as if all my senses have been heightened. I have no idea why, but it's one of those things that just is. Anyway, today, when Melissa started talking I saw a blurry female figure standing next to her, and yes, it looked like a ghost."

Her face was so pale and earnest, Marty had no choice but to take her seriously. "Okay. If I accept that, can you tell me what the ghost said, if anything?"

Laura was quiet for a little while then she answered. "She didn't say anything, it was more like I sensed what she wanted to say."

"And that was what?"

She looked away and then back at Marty. "The ghost-like...being... was telling me that Melissa didn't have long to live, and there was nothing I could do about it, but we would be involved. She said I would need to draw on all my psychic senses in the next few days."

Marty rolled her eyes. "Swell. That's just swell. You're telling me the woman I'm going to be meeting with is going to die. Is that what you're saying?"

Laura stared back at her. "I'm simply relating what the sense was that she gave me."

"Laura, I know you have abilities that the rest of us don't have, and I fully accept that. I don't understand it, but I'll give it to you, but now you're asking me to believe you saw a ghost and the ghost gave you the sense that my client was going to die? Terrific. Oh, and did Casper the ghost have a name or was it just Casper?" she asked sarcastically.

"Marty, I'm just telling you what happened. You're the one who asked and no, it did not have a name, but I got the sense that it was Melissa's mother."

Marty looked at her in astonishment. "Seriously? Melissa's mother came and stood next to her and told you her daughter was going to die? And you expect me to believe that?"

Laura looked miserable. "Marty, you have to believe me. I had nothing to do with it. It just happened."

"Sure. Can't you close down those senses or do something to control them? I mean, seeing ghosts is just plain weird. Let's hope it was a one-time thing and won't ever happen again. More importantly, let's hope that whatever you sensed was wrong."

Marty finished her coffee and put her napkin on the table. "Enough of your woo-woo stuff. I need to go see Carl, and see if Melissa's one of his clients. He might be able to give me a heads up on some items I'll be appraising if he sold them to her. Let's get the check and leave." She motioned the waiter over to their table.

"What can I do for you?" the elderly waiter asked. Marty assumed he had been a waiter at Melvyn's since the place had opened. It had a reputation for employing waiters who had worked there for decades, spanning their whole careers.

"We're ready for the check," Marty said.

"It's already been taken care of by Miss Ross. She said to tell you she hoped you enjoyed your lunch."

"We certainly did," Laura said, "but we didn't expect her to pay for it."

"Miss Ross is one of our most generous patrons. Enjoy the rest of your day," the waiter said as he walked away from the table.

CHAPTER NINE

During the past few decades, Palm Springs had spread far south from its original downtown location and now the general Palm Springs area encompassed several sister cities such as Cathedral City, Palm Desert, Rancho Mirage, and La Quinta. The Palm Springs Antique Shoppe, owned by Carl Mitchell, had developed a reputation for superb antiques, and his customers had no problem driving from the outlying areas to see what new treasures he'd obtained since they'd last been in his shop. Over the years, Marty and Carl had developed a professional relationship, and they had become good friends.

Marty had never mentioned it to Carl, but she was pretty sure a lot of his customers came to the shop just to find out the latest tidbit of gossip, which Carl was famous for passing on to his customers. Carl rarely missed a chance to mingle with the who's who of Palm Springs, thus his endless supply of information about the latest scandals among his rich clientele, along with the best art and antiques for sale in the area.

The bell above the door of the Palm Springs Antique Shoppe jingled gently as Marty opened it. Even though there were several customers in his shop, Carl acknowledged her by holding up his index finger indicating he'd be with her shortly. She spent the time looking at the prices of the art and antiques he'd added since she'd last been in his shop, always on the lookout to see what price things were selling for. This was simply research for her profession, that of an art and antique appraiser.

When Carl had rung up the sale for the last customer and the shop was quiet, he walked over to Marty and gave her a big hug. "It's been way too long, but I always get concerned when you come in. Usually it means someone has died, or worse yet, been murdered. I hope that's not the case this time."

"No, Carl, for once I came in just to see what you have. I'm doing a large appraisal beginning Wednesday for a woman who specializes in California art and antiques, as well as collecting some Indian artifacts."

"Glad to hear it, and I'm guessing that you're going to do Melissa Ross' collection? Would I be right?" he asked, grinning at her.

Marty looked at him in disbelief. "How would you possibly know that? I just had lunch with her to get to know her and find out about her antiques."

"Marty, darling, there is very little that goes on in this town pertaining to the rich and famous that I don't know about. Just from your description of her collection, I knew it had to be her. She's a doll, really one of my favorite customers, and her collection is to die for."

"That good, huh?" Marty asked. "And since you've sold a lot of it to her, you should know, right?"

"Let's put it this way, sweetheart. You didn't hear it from me but Rhonda Taylor wishes Melissa Ross had never won that Mega Millions jackpot. Rhonda hates her, and I mean really hates her, because Melissa's collection is better than hers, and Melissa outbids her most of the time. I hear Rhonda's rich doctor husband has a little female entertainment on the side he's paying for in the form of a very, very expensive condominium, a Bentley, and some pretty important jewelry. Hear he's put Rhonda on an art and antique spending diet, and it's really eating at her because she can't compete with Melissa."

"Carl, how do you hear things like that?"

"Well, darling, Rhonda comes in here all the time to see if I have anything new, so she can get it before Melissa does. You know how my customers like to talk to me, and it just seems like one thing leads to another. Rhonda knows about hubby's little extracurricular hobby and she looks like she's about ready to kill him, his hobby, and Melissa. I mean if looks could kill, she'd be the poster child. I guess that auction in Los Angeles last week put her over the edge. Melissa got the prize of the night, a pristine A+ Granville Redmond painting that Rhonda was sure she could pick up on the cheap, because it was a late addition to the auction."

"Come on, Carl." Marty lowered her voice, even though there was no one else in the shop. "I hardly think what you just told me came from Rhonda."

"You'd be surprised at both the things people tell me and who tells it to me. One more tidbit for you regarding Melissa Ross. From what I hear she's also made a mortal enemy of Tammy Crawford. I was down with the flu Saturday night, so I couldn't attend the Charity for Children gala, but I guess that big donation Melissa made really put Tammy over the edge. I heard you were sitting next to her at the head table with that handsome detective husband of yours. What did you think?"

"I think the FBI and CIA probably both have you on their "A" list of people to get in touch with if they ever need information about someone. Yes, I was sitting next to her, and she seemed very upset, but several minutes later I noticed she went over to the table where Melissa was sitting and the two women embraced."

"Oh," he said dismissively. "That's just for show. Melissa better watch her step, because she's treading on the toes of two women who have made it their goal in life to be number one in their field. One in art and antiques, and the other in philanthropy. If I were her, like I said, I'd be watching my backside."

"Carl, I think you're being a little melodramatic." Marty picked up a piece of California pottery, inwardly wincing when she saw the steep price tag. She carefully set it down again, not wanting to buy it because she'd broken it. "Rhonda and Tammy might be jealous of Melissa, but I'd be surprised if either of them ever decided to do anything about it. After all, they both are way too high-profile."

"Darling, your Midwest naivete never fails to amaze me, but I guess that's part of your charm."

"Thank you, I guess. Anyway, if you have a few minutes why don't you enlighten me about the prices paid for some of the things I'm going to be seeing at Melissa's home."

"I'll get my ledger. That will save you some time. By the way, I don't know how extensive your appraisal is going to be, but I'd be happy to help with the jewelry. I know that's not your specialty. Back in a minute," he said as he opened the door to his office.

When he returned with his ledger book, he put pencil marks next to the items Melissa had bought from him, saving Marty hours in research time, as well as saving her client hundreds of dollars.

An hour and a half later, she closed the ledger and put her notebook and pen in her purse. "Carl, thank you so much. This has been a huge help. Tomorrow I can go through some auction records to see what the comparables are on similar items. You've really saved me hours of research, and I promise, if any jewelry is involved, I know who to ask to appraise it."

CHAPTER TEN

"Today's the day you start that big appraisal, right?" Jeff asked as he picked up his holster and secured it to his shoulder. "Last night you told us at dinner that Carl had been a huge help."

"He sure was. Saved me hours in research." Marty bent down to open the dishwasher, putting the breakfast dishes inside it. "I actually feel pretty good about this. Dick, Laura's boss at the insurance company, wanted Laura to go with me, so she could see the art and antiques. She's going to leave after we do a walk-through. Melissa was fine with it. I had a message from her yesterday that she had something she had to attend, so I'm going to meet her maid, Isabella, at the bottom of the driveway, and she'll let me into the house. Melissa told me at lunch that Isabella knows where everything is. I should be home around 5:30 or so, and you?" She closed the dishwasher and washed her hands.

"Same old, same old. I'm working on a couple of cold cases. The chief has us do that when things are a little slow."

"By a little slow, you mean when no murders have happened? Guess that must be an inside joke or something. Somehow having things be a little slow and investigating murders don't seem like the two should go together," Marty said as she approached him and lightly kissed his cheek.

"You're right. Don't think the victim's relatives would like that particular way of phrasing it. I'll be a little more careful from now on," he said grinning.

"Think that would be wise, Detective," she said as she opened the door and walked out. As soon as she was in the courtyard, Patron ran up to her, barking and turning in circles. She stopped and said, "Hey, little guy, what's the problem?"

Just then Jeff followed her out of the house and started walking towards where his car was parked. "I've got to go, Marty," Jeff said. "See if you can calm him down. If he keeps barking it's bound to affect Les' work on his latest painting, and I don't think our buddy Les will be very happy about it. See you tonight."

"Morning, Sis," Laura said, walking out of her house to meet Marty. "Is that Patron I hear?"

"Yes, he's really agitated, and I have no idea why."

"It's kind of like what he was doing the other night," Laura said. "I don't understand what's up with him, but I'm sure Les won't be happy with it. He does his best work when all of us are gone, but if Patron continues to bark, that's not going to please him. Let me see if I can calm this little fella down."

Laura sat down beside the young dog and whispered to him. Marty stood a few feet away from them, and within minutes, she noticed that Patron had become calm and he'd stopped barking. Laura continued to quietly talk to him.

I wonder if she's doing some psychic mumbo-jumbo, Marty thought, *but whatever she's doing, it seems to be working.*

"Okay, Marty, I think he's quieted down enough that we can leave for Melissa's. I'll follow you in my car."

They walked over to the gate, Patron following behind. When Marty pulled out of the driveway, she looked over and saw Patron watching her, his nose at the gate, taking Duke's place, who was now behind Patron. Marty didn't know what had transpired, but some type of communication had definitely passed between Laura and Patron and then between Patron and Duke. Whatever it was, she wasn't in on it.

*****

Marty followed the directions Melissa had given her and turned onto a tree-lined avenue that led to several homes which backed up to the nearby mountains. The mid-20th century homes blended into the mountains they nestled against. The lots and the homes were huge, and in keeping with the desert, all had been landscaped with drought-tolerant plants.

When they had lunch, Melissa had told Marty and Laura that the residents of that part of Palm Springs had bought there because of the way the architects had blended the homes into the mountain terrain and had decided not to have fences or guard gates. They felt it would destroy the sense of being one with nature, which was one of the reasons they'd chosen to buy in that area, rather than in the newer gate-guarded communities. Melissa had laughed and said her attorney had hounded her to get a gun and go to the shooting range if she was going to live there because, even though the Palm Springs police regularly patrolled the area, simply by looking at the homes, it was apparent people of means lived there.

Melissa had told her that in keeping with the original architecture, she had chosen to keep the turquoise front door, a feature of many of the homes built during that timeframe in the desert. Marty easily found the house and as she approached, she saw a woman who she assumed was Isabella, waiting for her at the end of a long driveway. She motioned for the woman to get in the car.

"Hi, I'm Marty. You must be Isabella. Melissa left a message for me that you would be waiting for me. My sister is in the car behind us. Is it okay if we park in the driveway? She's just going to be here for a few minutes."

"*Si,*" Isabella said softly.

Marty looked over at her and noticed that she was wringing her hands together, as if she was worried or distressed.

What do I know? She's Melissa's maid, not mine, and everyone's different. Maybe she's having some problems at home.

Marty parked her car in the driveway. Laura parked behind Marty's car and Marty introduced her to Isabella as they walked up to the front door. Isabella took a keychain with several keys on it from her purse and opened the front door which led to a tiled entryway.

"Please, go ahead," Isabella said. "I will show you Miss Ross' art and antiques. You can put your purses here in the hallway on this bench. We can begin in the living room."

Laura looked over at Marty and raised her eyebrows as if to say, "Why is her voice quivering?" They set their purses down, and Marty took what she'd need for her appraisal out of a large brown leather tote, which included her tape recorder, a tape measure, a notebook, and her camera. She wore a magnifying loupe around her neck. She often thought she hadn't come out of her first marriage with much, but she did love the magnifying glass which was surrounded by diamonds and gold filigree suspended on a heavy gold chain. It was something her former husband had given her when she'd become a certified antique appraiser.

"Okay, I'm ready," Marty said, as she followed Isabella towards what she assumed was the living room. The doors were closed and Isabella opened them, then stepped back, as if in deference, letting Marty and Laura enter the room first.

They took one step into the room and stopped, staring in open-mouthed shock at the body of Melissa Ross sprawled on the floor. Melissa's eyes were lifeless, and it was apparent that not only would she not be buying any antiques in the future, neither would she be attending any charitable events.

"What is it?" Isabella asked in a shaky voice. She walked around them and screamed. *"Madre de Dios!"* She crossed herself with her right hand. "She's dead, I know she's dead."

Marty bent down and put her fingers on both sides of Melissa's neck. There was no pulse. She stood up and walked back to where she'd put her purse. With her hands shaking, she held her cell phone and pressed in Jeff's number. A moment later she heard his voice in her ear. "Marty, I thought you were doing that appraisal this morning. Is everything okay?"

In a trembling voice that matched Isabella's of just moments earlier, she said, "Jeff, Melissa's dead." She told him how they'd discovered Melissa lying on the floor in the living room right after they arrived.

She was relieved when Jeff took control. "Tell Laura and the maid not to touch a thing. We'll be there within five minutes."

Isabella continued to sob loudly, interspersed with words of Spanish. Laura and Marty tried to console her, without much success. Marty noticed that Laura had become pale and wondered if she was having another "visitation." That was the only word Marty could think of to describe what she'd witnessed at the restaurant the day before yesterday. It seemed to happen whenever Laura was in Melissa's presence. Within minutes Jeff and other first responders filled the room.

Jeff put his arms around Marty. "Are you all right?"

"Yes, I'm fine," she answered, resting her head on his chest before looking back up at him. "What do you think happened? Maybe she had a heart attack, but she seems way too young for that to happen."

"I have no idea. I'm going to have one of my men take a statement from each of you. While you're doing that, I'll see what I can find out."

Marty pulled away just as Jeff started barking orders to his team. A policewoman efficiently started to put yellow crime scene tape around the house as the various police experts began to search the rooms for clues. The crime scene became a hub of activity as photos were taken, people spoke into recorders and the coroner's team secured the body for the trip to the county morgue.

"Jeff, I've given my statement to your detective. I have a meeting at 10:00 with Dick and some important new clients. Would it be okay if I leave now?" Laura asked her brother-in-law.

"Yes. There's nothing more for you to do here." He looked closely at her. "Laura, you're really pale. Do you feel up to driving? If not, I can have one of my men take you to your office."

Laura shook her head and mustered an unsteady smile. "No, I'm all right. I'll tell you all about it tonight. Jeff, she was murdered. Start there." With that, Laura walked down the hall, retrieved her purse, and left the house.

Jeff walked over to where Marty was still trying to console Isabella. "Marty, may I see you for a moment?" She followed him down the hall. "Do you know what's up with Laura? She was absolutely white and shaking. I offered to have one of my men drive her to her office, but she said she was okay, and she'd tell me all about it tonight. She also said that Melissa was murdered and to start there. I did notice what looked like a puncture wound on her arm, but there's nothing else I can see that would suggest she was murdered. Maybe Laura saw it too, and that's what she was talking about."

"I have an idea, but it can wait until I see you later," Marty said. "I don't think I should try to appraise anything until this is no longer an active crime scene. Of course, Laura will tell Dick when she gets to the office, but I need to find out what he wants me to do now. Maybe he has the name of her lawyer, and we can find something out there. I told Isabella I'd take her home, since she rides the bus to work. Is it okay if the two of us leave now?"

"Yes. There's nothing more you can do here. I'll see you tonight."

*****

"I can certainly understand why you're upset, Isabella," Marty said as she pulled her car up at the address of the apartment Isabella had given her. It was in a part of Palm Springs that wasn't on the tourist maps. It looked like every other run-down type of neighborhood that's seen in urban areas of the United States. Abandoned cars, appliances, and mattresses filled the vacant lot next to the building that was clearly in need of some tender loving care.

Dirt scattered with litter had replaced the grass that had once grown in the front yard which was split in half by a cracked and broken sidewalk. The front door to the building was covered with graffiti as was the lower part of the building. It was obvious the only residents who inhabited the building were too poor to go anywhere else.

"My husband is the chief detective who came to the house," Marty said. "He'll probably know something tomorrow about whether or not you should go back to work there. I don't know if Miss Ross had any relatives, but if not, I imagine the house will be sold and whoever is the executor of her estate may want you to stay until it's sold. Why don't you call Jeff tomorrow? Here's his card. Again, I'm sorry for your loss."

"*Gracias*," Isabella said, wiping tears from her eyes. "You are very kind. I will call him tomorrow. I don't know what to do now. If someone wants me to stay on for a while, I will have to get my keys back. The police took them."

"I'm sure that can be arranged. I'll let Jeff know."

CHAPTER ELEVEN

The compound was quiet when Marty returned home. The only visible activity was two sets of tails wagging at the front gate, eagerly anticipating her return. She let the dogs out and smiled, thinking how the two dogs had nothing more to do or think about than chasing one another in the desert or finding some type of critter, perhaps a lizard, moving on the hot desert floor. She walked a short distance into the desert with them as they scampered about.

"Okay, guys, time to go back," Marty said. "Since I have a little free time I'm going to use it to good advantage and finish reading the appraisal that June sent me. I want to make sure she was able to transcribe my descriptions, because the television was blaring the whole time I was appraising, making me lose my train of thought on several occasions."

The dogs happily followed her into the house, walked over to their dog beds, and promptly went to sleep. She changed into a casual outfit consisting of a loose gauzy white top over khaki cotton pants. Given the shocking events of the morning, she didn't feel like eating lunch and started in on the packet June had sent her. June had also sent her the appraisal as an attachment to her email, well aware that Marty liked to edit a print copy and then use that to correct the digital copy for final preparation. Marty knew that most appraisers didn't take the extra print copy step, but she felt it was essential. Too many times her brain had told her a word was there when it wasn't.

Several hours had passed by when Marty heard voices coming from the courtyard. She glanced at the bottom of her computer screen and realized it was 5:30, the time the residents of the compound started to congregate outside to share a bottle of wine, one of John's fabulous dinners, and catch up on the events of the day. Marty fed the dogs and walked over to the long table where John, Max, Laura, and Les were seated.

"I peeked in on you a little while ago," Laura said, "but you were concentrating so hard, I didn't want to interrupt. Hear anything from Jeff?" she asked.

Before Marty could answer, the gate opened and a deep voice said, "I heard that, and no, she did not. I was waiting until I got home to share an update. And Laura, I want to talk to you. Give me a minute to change."

"Yeah, I had the television on in the Pony while I was prepping lunch," John said, "and I heard that Melissa Ross had been murdered. Figured Jeff caught the investigation. So, you two were also involved?" He turned to where Marty was now sitting beside her sister.

"Yes, we were," Marty said. "Actually, Laura and I were the ones who discovered her body. I was supposed to start an appraisal there today, but I'm on hold at the moment." Marty gave the group a brief recap of the scene she and Laura had encountered on their visit to Melissa's home that morning.

Jeff walked up to the table as she finished and poured himself a glass of wine. "Cheers," he said, holding up his glass, "although my day wasn't one to celebrate. I need to give Marty some direction on the appraisal, and I can also tell you what happened on the case. It will be public information pretty soon if it isn't already."

"I'm all ears," John said. "Dinner is on hold, but I think I was able to create those appetizers you had at the gala. I'll get them and you can tell me what you think. Don't start without me." A few minutes later he returned with a platter in his hands and passed it around.

"Well, Marty, Jeff? What do you think? Pretty close to what you had?"

"Better, definitely better," Marty said, wiping a crumb from the side of her mouth. "These are delicious."

"Agreed, John. Nice job." Jeff took another stuffed mushroom and popped it in his mouth. "Okay, here's what we have so far. There was a puncture wound on the victim's body. The coroner thinks she was probably poisoned, but has no idea by what. He said he needed to do some research on it, because none of the usual signs of the type of poisons he's familiar with were present."

"Is that a good thing or a bad thing?" Les asked, his mouth full of a shrimp and grits puff pastry.

"Les, didn't your mother ever tell you not to talk with your mouth full?" Laura asked.

"She did, and she also told me to never try to make a career of painting. When I sold my first painting for more money than my college education had cost, I threw out all the mother knows best things. Mother definitely didn't know what was best for me."

"To answer your question, Les," Jeff answered, "it can go either way. If the poison is something rare and difficult to obtain, that could help us find the murderer by trying to locate who would have access to such a substance. Then again, it could be so rare that there are no similar cases to go by, and that would definitely be a bad thing."

He turned to Marty. "We'll be finishing up with the crime scene tomorrow. I spoke with Melissa's attorney, and he wants you to go ahead with the appraisal. He said he'll need it when it comes time to distribute the estate, and he said he would use the values you establish."

"Okay," Marty said as she reached for another mushroom and then continued, "Jeff, I took Isabella home and naturally, she's pretty shaken by this. Did the attorney say anything about her continuing to work in the house? I have no way to get in, and she mentioned that the police had taken her keys. Know anything about that?"

"Yes, he said Melissa's trust stipulates that the house is to be sold upon her death. She made a special bequest to Isabella and said that she is to continue working in the house and be paid until the sale of the house is complete. I called her this afternoon and told her you'd be meeting her the day after tomorrow at the end of the driveway, the same place you met her this morning. The house is off limits tomorrow, so I'll give you her keys and you can return them to her."

"Jeff, I understand Melissa Ross was the winner of a Mega Millions jackpot," Les said. "I've read articles in the paper about her, but there was little mention of any family. I think one article I read said something about her being raised by an uncle outside of Barstow, because both of her parents had died at a young age."

"That's true, Les. In her trust and will she specifically disinherits her uncle and her brother, if, in fact, either one of them is living at the time of her death. She had no other relatives. Tomorrow I'll start with the actual investigation and have one of my men working on finding out if either one of them is alive, and if so, where they are, because they could possibly be considered suspects in her murder."

"Jeff," Marty said, "you used the word murder. Is that official or your take on it?"

"Until the coroner's report comes back, it's my take on it, but I think it's pretty solid. Before it's officially called murder, he needs to rule out natural causes, but everyone is pretty sure she didn't die from natural causes." Jeff turned towards Laura. "So, dear sister-in-law, what caused you to be so pale today? Have another ghost sighting, did you?" he asked with a twinkle in his eye.

"Sorry, Jeff, as a matter of fact I did." The table became completely quiet as the others turned and looked at Laura. "I know you'll ask for a full description, so here's what I saw, or more accurately, sensed." She closed her eyes for a moment, and Marty could tell she was deep breathing. "There was a pale, ghost-like figure next to Melissa's body," Laura said eventually. "Actually, the figure was kind of surrounding Melissa like she was trying to protect her. It was as if I could hear words coming from the shape, or aura, but of course I couldn't. It was more like I sensed the ghost, for lack of a better word, saying 'Someday, someday. I knew when she won the money it would happen someday. I just didn't know when or how. All these years I've been able to protect her, but not this time. I didn't have the antidote.' And Jeff, it's like I absorbed the words rather than having them spoken to me. I didn't hear them through my ears."

Jeff was quiet for several moments, as they all were. "Coming from anyone but you, Laura, I'd be rolling on the floor with laughter. Please notice I'm not laughing. Do you think the ghost was talking about people from the past or the present?"

"I wish I could tell you, Jeff, but I have no idea. What difference would that make? Murder is murder."

"Yes, it is, but it sure would help me in my investigation. According to the attorney, she had a brother and an uncle. What if they didn't know she'd disinherited them, and one of them killed her? What if it was someone who knew her after she became rich." He turned to Marty. "Remember how angry Tammy Crawford was about the donation Melissa gave to the Charity for Children?"

"Jeff, you may be onto something. I didn't mention it last night, but I stopped by my friend Carl's antique shop after Laura, Melissa, and I finished lunch the other day." She told them about her conversation with Carl and his gossip about Rhonda Taylor.

"Stop right there," John said. "I think I peaked with my appetizers and the desserts tonight. You've already sampled the appetizers, but for dessert you have a choice of Jack and Coke cake or a butterscotch brownie with caramel sauce, both of which, may I add, are scrumptious. For the main course we're having a skillet sausage pasta, because I was tired from cooking the rest of the meal. It's time to serve it. Don't say anything more, and I'll be back in a minute. Come on, Max," He motioned to his co-worker. "I could use a couple more hands."

The table was quiet as they enjoyed the meal, the silence broken when all of them heaped accolades on John, not only for the desserts, but also for the sausage pasta. Everyone said it was really unusual and understood why it was such a hit with his customers at The Red Pony.

Max brought out a tray with a coffee pot, mugs, cream and sugar on it. "Help yourself. Didn't think anyone would want to leave until we hear what Jeff's plans are for the investigation, if you can tell us," he said nodding towards Jeff.

"I've been thinking about it while we've been eating. We should know something more definitive about the cause of death by tomorrow, so we'll probably get some additional information there. As I mentioned, presently we're looking into the whereabouts of the brother and uncle, if they're even alive." He turned to Marty.

"I know I tell you how I don't want you to get involved in my cases, but since you were the one, along with your sister, who discovered the body, I have a thought on how you might be able to help me."

Marty looked up. "Of course, what would you like me to do?"

Jeff stirred his coffee before lifting the cup and taking a sip. "It involves Carl. Do you think he'd be game for a little sleuthing?"

"As much as he likes to be involved in what the rich and famous are doing, I'm sure he'd love to be involved," Marty said with a laugh. "What do you have in mind?"

"I'd like him to call Rhonda Taylor and tell her that you're a friend of his, and he happened to mention that she had the best art and antique collections in the area. Tell him you'd like him to ask her if he could bring you to her home to see her collections. For the most part collectors love to show off their collections, or so you've told me, so I'm hoping she'd be game. When you're with her, you might just happen to mention that you were going to do an appraisal of the Ross collection and did she know anything about it? Play dumb. You can say that it's been delayed because of her death. I'm more interested in seeing if you can find anything out or sense anything."

Marty considered the idea. "Sure. I'll call Carl tomorrow morning. Knowing him, we'll probably have an appointment set up with her by the afternoon. The people who do business with him absolutely love him. I also had a thought during dinner. Tammy gave me her business card the other night and said since I dealt with a lot of rich people, maybe I could send someone her way who could make a donation to one of the charities she's involved in.

"I was thinking I could call her and tell her I have an idea for getting more donations for her charities. I could donate my services for a complimentary art and antique appraisal. I'd have to set up some parameters, so I don't get stuck doing a two-week appraisal for free. Maybe like a day or two or just one collection. That way, I could talk to her and see if I get a sense of anything there."

"That's a great plan." Jeff turned back to Laura. "Have you ever seen this ghost, or whatever it was, other than when you've been with Melissa?"

Laura was quiet for several long moments and then said, "No, I haven't. I have a sense it was someone who's trying to protect Melissa. Something occurred to me that may sound pretty strange. Melissa told us at lunch that her mother always said the word 'someday' as when she would have the beautiful things she wanted or enough money to donate. The ghost, for lack of a better term, used that same word. I think that's a little strange. I'm wondering if the ghost is her mother, and has been protecting her." She took a sip from her cup and sat back, steeling herself for what she was afraid they would say, possibly even thoughts concerning her mental state. Given the long relationship she'd had with Les, his was the opinion she most valued. Fortunately, her fears were unfounded.

"Laura, I think you may have something," Les said. "I know things happen in life that can't be explained rationally. They certainly do to you, and I say that in all honesty. I've seen them. With your perceptive powers, Melissa's mother's spirit may feel comfortable with you. Yes, I very much think it could be her mother."

"Well, what I'm going to say next has nothing to do with police protocols," Jeff said, "but here goes. I think this ghost has things to tell you, Laura, things that may help solve this murder mystery. I think the ghost will only talk or communicate in whatever way you want to call it, with you." Jeff took a deep breath and continued, "I know I'm going out on a limb here, but would you be willing to go to the coroner's office tomorrow and see if you can contact the ghost?" He shook his head in surprise. "Man, I can't believe I even just said that. I hope to heck the chief never hears about it, because I'll definitely deny it."

All eyes were now on Laura. She again seemed deep in thought for several moments and then she spoke up. "Yes, I feel certain the ghost has things to tell me. Keep in mind that the two times I've seen the ghost, other people were around. I'm going even further out on the limb here. Could you arrange for me to be alone with Melissa's body?"

It was Jeff's turn to be quiet for a few moments, and then he said, "The coroner and I have had some conversations in the past about strange things. He's from New Orleans and mentioned once that his mother was what they call a conjure doctor. He said it's part of the practice of hoodoo and that it involves mysticism and things of that nature.

"He went on to tell me how I'd never believe the things his mother could do. She was born the seventh daughter of a seventh daughter, and sons or daughters who are the seventh from the seventh are the ones designated to carry on the practice. Someone came into the room when we were talking that day and our conversation was interrupted, but I think he'd be willing to look the other way, although he's not supposed to ever leave a corpse alone with someone. Definitely against procedure. Anyway, I'll go see him tomorrow and let you know what he says. And once again, Laura, I owe you. Thank you, and if nothing comes of it, I'll at least know I tried. I'd always wonder what would have happened if I didn't let you give it a shot."

CHAPTER TWELVE

"Hi, Carl," Marty said when he answered her phone call to him the following morning. "Bear with me, but I have a rather odd request for you. First of all, have you ever thought you'd like to be involved in solving a crime?"

"Of course." Carl chuckled at the other end of the line. "I have my very own Superman cape in the closet just waiting to be called so it can be taken out and put into action. Every boy and man wants to do that, but Marty, you're already making me nervous. I'll never forget how your sister brought that big kitchen knife into the bedroom, sliced through the Styrofoam wig stand, and pulled out that missing diamond ring. Darling, I have to tell you if it involves Laura and that woo-woo stuff she does, the answer might very well be no. Let me ask you a question. Does this have anything to do with the death of Melissa Ross?"

Marty sighed. "You're never going to let me forget that wig stand episode, are you? Almost every time I see you, you bring it up. No, Carl, Laura is not involved in this, although it may have something to do with Melissa's death."

At least Laura's not involved in what I'm going to ask you to do, and she won't be with us, Marty thought, internally justifying her response.

"You told me about Rhonda Taylor when I stopped by your shop the other day," she continued, "and how she more or less defines herself as being the top art and antique collector in the Palm Springs area. I'd like to meet her. I was thinking maybe you could call her and tell her that you have a good friend who's an appraiser, and you were telling me that she had the best art and antique collection in the area. That should feed her ego. Anyway, I'd like you to ask her if you could show me her collection, and the sooner the better."

"I can do you one better than that, Marty. I have a perfect excuse to go there. She bought quite a few pieces at the auction Tuesday night, although your deceased client got the best of them," he said with a catty undertone. "Unfortunately, 1 couldn't attend the auction. Anyway, I can tell her I'd like to see the new additions to her collection. She and I talked last week about the auction, so it would be very natural for me to want to see what she got."

"I was hoping you would say something like that," Marty said with a smile. She looked out the window to where Duke and Patron were frolicking in the courtyard. As if they could sense her looking at them, they turned and approached the door.

"Knowing Rhonda, her ego is so tied up in her collections, I'm sure she'll invite us over," Carl was saying. "I'll call her this morning and get back to you. I'll see what I can do to get us in to see her collections as soon as possible. Are you available this afternoon?"

"Yes. Thanks, Carl. I'll wait to hear from you." She ended the call and went over to the door where the two dogs were standing. "Think it's time for a little walk in the desert. What do you say, guys?"

The answer to her question was two tails enthusiastically being wagged. Now that Duke had shed his aversion to putting his feet on the desert floor, and they'd been able to get rid of his pink booties, he loved to go see what kind of interesting things he could smell and see with Patron right behind him. And if a dog was lucky he might just be able to find a lizard to chase. The possibilities were endless.

When the three of them returned to Marty's house, her answer machine indicated she had a message. A moment later she heard

Carl's voice say, "Marty, we're in luck. We have an appointment at Rhonda's at 4:00 p.m. today. Why don't you come to the shop about 3:45? She just lives a short distance from here. If I don't hear back from you, I'll see you then. By the way, I took my cape out of the closet, but I think I better put it in my briefcase, rather than wear it. Might frighten poor Rhonda."

The picture of Carl in a Superman outfit made Marty laugh out loud, causing both of the dogs to look at her. Marty didn't laugh out loud very much when she was by herself, and the dogs always noticed anything that was different. "Sorry, guys. Didn't mean to make you nervous. I was just enjoying a moment of levity." They seemed to understand and retreated to their dog beds to take their morning nap.

She took the card Tammy Crawford had given her out of her desk drawer and spent a few moments deciding exactly what she wanted to say to her when she called. When she was ready, she picked up her phone and pressed in the numbers.

"Crawford residence. May I help you?" asked the voice on the other end of the phone.

"Yes, this is Marty Morgan. My husband, Detective Jeff Combs, and I were seated at Mrs. Crawford's table at the Charity for Children event. She asked me to call her if I knew of anyone who wanted to make a donation to one of her charities."

"Certainly. I'll get Mrs. Crawford. Please hold."

A moment later a smooth voice said, "Marty, how nice to hear from you. How can I help you?"

"I've been thinking about the wonderful work you do, and came up with an idea for a silent auction donation that I think might appeal to the people who attend galas, such as the one the other night. I was wondering if you'd be free to see me early this afternoon so I can tell you about my idea?" Marty held her breath, waiting for Tammy's response.

"Yes, that should work. I have a luncheon meeting, but I should be home by 2:00. Why don't you come to the house at 2:30, and we can talk then? Here's my address. It's an estate in the older part of town. You know, the part of town where the movie stars built homes when Palm Springs became the 'in' place. A lot of us prefer the elegance and class from that era to the newer cookie-cutter gate-guarded communities the snowbirds like so much," she said with an air of haughtiness.

Marty wrote down the address. "Thank you for agreeing to see me on such short notice. I'm going to be busy for the next few days, and I wanted to take care of this before I forgot about it. See you at 2:30," she said, ending the call.

She pulled Google Maps up on her laptop computer and saw that the address Tammy had given her wasn't far from Carl's antique shop.

Rather interesting that Rhonda and Melissa both lived relatively close to Tammy, she mused. *Must be a status symbol thing, living in one of the original areas of Palm Springs, although from what I saw when Jeff and I went to La Quinta the other night, I think I could be very happy in one of those areas.*

Just then she heard a little voice in the back of her head saying, *"Who are you kidding? There's no way you could be happy there, Marty. That's why you love it up here in High Desert, away from the Botoxed women, the fancy cars, and the bling you see so much of in the Palm Springs area."*

She quieted the voice by reminding herself that those were the very people who needed her services as an art and antique appraiser, and if that went with the job, she could deal with it as long as she could return to her home in the High Desert compound she'd grown to love.

CHAPTER THIRTEEN

Marty wasn't quite sure how one was supposed to dress when going to the homes of two of the most influential women in Palm Springs. One, the queen of the philanthropists, and the other, the grand duchess of art and antique collecting. She decided to go for a subdued desert look, which she hoped would be sophisticated enough for Tammy Crawford and Rhonda Taylor's high standards.

A few minutes later she looked in the mirror and thought the short-sleeved light blue silk blouse and dark blue silk pants would pass inspection. She took a pearl necklace and matching earrings out of her jewelry box, smiling as she thought of how rarely she wore them, and how much pleasure they'd given her mother.

She made sure the dogs had plenty of water and that they could get out into the courtyard through the doggie door. Almost year-round air-conditioning was a necessity in the desert and leaving doors and windows open was not an option.

Marty realized it was still too early to leave for her appointments, so she decided to stop by the Hi-Lo Drugstore. Whenever she did an appraisal, she took extensive photographs of the items she was appraising. The photos were necessary to verify size, color, or any damage of the items being appraised. She took the photos to the Hi-Lo Drugstore to be developed into hard copy prints which were then attached to the final copy of her appraisal.

The photographs she had developed at the Hi-Lo were always a crucial element of her appraisals. She knew that the attorney for the Ross estate, as well as Dick at the insurance company, would want her to do the Ross appraisal as soon as possible. The woman who worked in the photo department at the drugstore, Lucy, had become a good friend of Marty's. She wanted to talk to Lucy and make sure she could get the photos she would need developed without any delay.

When Marty opened the door to the drugstore, she waved at Lucy, who was with a customer. Lucy was telling the customer in her own version of the English language when the man could expect to receive his photographs.

"Sir, ain't no way I can do 'em as fast as 'ya want 'em done. I'm as busy as a tick on a coon most of the time, so I gotta' send 'em down to the Springs. Got some fancy development shop down there. Most times I gets 'em back in a day or so, but can't make ya' no firm promises. That's just the way it is." She folded her arms across her chest and set her mouth in a straight line.

Marty could tell by the way the customer looked at Lucy that he was new to the area. The regulars had all experienced delays because of the high-tech photo developing shop in Palm Springs. Marty always wondered why the Hi-Lo didn't hire someone to develop the prints and do it in-house. She'd finally reached the conclusion it was one of those things that just is, and it was never going to be other than that. A few minutes later the man walked away with a puzzled expression on his face.

"Lady, get over here. Got a bone to pick with ya'," Lucy said. "Why didn't ya' tell me you gots ya' a new little one?"

"Lucy, I'm sorry, but you've lost me. What are you talking about?"

"Talkin' 'bout that new little addition to the Combs family. Hear from my source that his name is Patron and he's 'bout cute as a bug's ear."

The corners of Marty's mouth turned up. "Who told you that, Lucy? Has anyone from the compound been in recently?"

"Nah, yer' the only one of the group that comes in. Oh, once in a while that sister of yers' does for some allergy thing, but never see the menfolk. Heard it from Mel, you know, the mailman. Says that handsome husband of yers' was walkin' that cute l'il bundle of white and tol' him it was a gift from him to ya'. How come ya' never mentioned it?" she said, assuming a mock belligerent stance with her hands on her hips.

"I'm sorry, Lucy, it never occurred to me, and the last few times I've been in here, the only thing that's been on my mind were the photographs I needed for one of my appraisals." Marty seriously doubted the mailman had described Jeff as handsome and assumed that was Lucy's own opinion. Maybe that was why Jeff never came in the Hi-Lo.

"Well, girl, in that case, guess I can forgive ya', but only on one condition. Wanna' see a picture of that l'il guy. If'n yer' like me, you'll have a bunch of 'em in yer' purse."

"Lucy, I don't have a bunch of them, but I did put one in my wallet. Let me get it." She reached in her purse, opened her wallet, and said, "Here's a recent photo of Patron." She passed it over to Lucy.

Lucy studied it intently and totally surprised Marty by saying, "L'il guy got the gene, don't he?"

"I have no idea what you're talking about. What gene?"

"That thing that makes him special, like he's got some, think it's called, supernatural gift. Read an article in one of them dog magazines my ol' man brought home. He went to the library when we got Killer to figger out the best way to train him. Between you and me, don't think it did much good, cuz' Killer definitely knows we follow him, rather than the other way 'round."

Lucy leaned in towards Marty and spoke in hushed tones, as if she was telling her a secret. "Anyway, this article said somethin' 'bout dogs with eyes like yer' l'il guy got this ability. They know things that are gonna' happen, like. I read a coupla' stories 'bout dogs that predicted who won the Kentucky Derby and 'nother one who was able to predict whether a pregnant woman was gonna have her a boy or a girl. Yup, ya' got a special one there." Lucy gave her a knowing wink.

For one of the few times in her life, Marty was speechless. She simply didn't know what to say, but as she processed what Lucy had just told her, she wondered if Patron did have some sort of a special gift. Maybe that was why he'd barked before the gala and yesterday before she and Laura discovered Melissa's body.

It appeared Lucy wasn't quite done with her words of wisdom. "Think I tol' you once that I get a quote or some sayin' from different places every day and kinda' like to think about it durin' the day. I always get the ones that make me feel good. Guess some people would call them inspirational. Anyway, was playin' 'round with Pinterest this morning before I came to work and got this one."

She took a piece of paper out of her purse and unfolded it. "Ya' ready?" she asked.

"Yes, although this conversation is taking me into some unknown territory," Marty said.

"Well, jes' thinkin' it's real weird that you come in here today with a picture of that l'il guy and my thought for the day is this: 'The eternal being, as it lives in us, also lives in every animal.' Some guy named Arthur Shopenhauer was the one who said it. Don't that beat all? You jes' keep an eye on that l'il guy and you'll learn some things. I'd bet everythin' I got on it, course that ain't much. Jes' too concidental, if you ask me." Lucy folded the paper again into a small square and put it back in her purse.

"Lucy, I think the word is coincidental, but I know what you're saying. I'll keep it in mind. You may be right."

"Nah, darlin', I know I'm right. All you need to do is look in them eyes. Them ain't the eyes of Killer, I'll tell ya' that."

I still can't believe Lucy's husband named that sweet little yellow Labrador retriever, Killer, Marty thought to herself.

"Lucy, I have an appointment, and I need to leave. Other than to say hi to you, the reason I came in here today was to see what your workload is looking like for the next few days. I'm starting an appraisal tomorrow, and I'm going to want as quick a turnaround as you can do on my photos."

"Darlin', for you, no prob. It's guys like the one ya' just saw that got's the problem. I always put a big sign on yer' stuff that says, 'Special Handling, Lucy', and ol' Derek down at the developin' place puts it in front of all the others. Fer you, a one-day turnaround, but jes' don't go blabbin' 'bout it, ya' hear?" She glanced around to check that no one was listening, even though her booming voice was hard to miss.

"I promise, Lucy, thanks. And thanks for the information about Patron. Could be. He has barked a couple of times before things have happened, and that could be the reason. I really do need to leave. I'll probably just upload the photos to you rather than come by personally. Would that be okay?"

"Sure. No prob. Good luck with that dead woman you discovered."

Marty was taken aback. "Lucy, where did you hear anything about that?"

"Got my sources, darlin', got my sources." Lucy tapped the side of her nose with her forefinger. "Lookin' forward to seein' them new pretty pics of yers'. Talk to ya' later."

CHAPTER FOURTEEN

After Marty left the Hi-Lo Drugstore, she found herself thinking about what Lucy had said regarding Patron. She knew Lucy was a gossip, and she didn't want Patron and his gift, if he had one, bandied about with all her customers. The more she thought about it, the more she thought Lucy might be right. That would explain Patron's barking and growling, and it would also explain Laura's ability to calm him down. She already knew that Laura thought the dog was psychic.

The address Tammy had given her was only a couple of streets over from Melissa's home, and she easily drove to it. In contrast to Melissa's home, which had fit into the landscape, Tammy's home was pure Southwest style from its red tile roof to the inset tiles on the white stucco wall enclosing the front patio. Black wrought iron grillwork in the shape of a cross covered each window, presumably to prevent anyone from breaking into the home. It reminded Marty of the grillwork partially covering the windows at the La Quinta resort.

Marty parked her car in the driveway and walked up to the black grillwork gate. She pressed the intercom button on the side of it and heard a voice telling her that the gate was unlocked, and Mrs. Crawford would meet her at the front door. As she approached the large wraparound porch, the front door opened and Tammy appeared. "It's good to see you again, Marty. Come in. I thought we could talk in my office. Please follow me."

As they walked down the hall, Marty was surprised by the way the home was furnished. There was nothing in it that matched the exterior. The furnishings were very high end European furniture with Oriental rugs and French, German, and Italian decorative objects.

"Tammy, I'm somewhat surprised at your choice of interior décor and furniture, given the Southwestern style of your home. Quite frankly, I expected to see Native American rugs on the floor and other Southwest art and artifacts. Instead, it looks like almost everything you have is European and of a very high quality. The Oriental rugs look authentic and are exquisite."

"Thank you," Tammy said, stopping and making a sweeping gesture with her hand. "Almost everything in our home came from my husband's family. They were very wealthy, as you can imagine, since I'm such a large donor to various charitable organizations. I may have mentioned that to you previously."

"I think you did," Marty murmured.

"Lew's family gave us a number of pieces when we were married," Tammy went on, "as did his grandparents, and then when his parents died, as an only child, he inherited everything. I've often thought I'd like to sell some of the things, so I could give even more to my philanthropic interests."

Marty followed her down the hall. "How fortunate you are to live with such beautiful things," Marty said. "I know many of my clients would love to have these things if you do decide to sell some of them."

"Please have a seat," Tammy said as they entered her office. Marty stood for a moment, hardly believing her eyes. All four walls were covered with photographs and articles either about or including Tammy Crawford. If Marty had ever wondered if people had been right when they said Tammy considered the most important thing in her life to be her philanthropic work, the room dispelled all doubt. She felt like she was in some kind of a shrine, and the goddess prayed to here was Tammy, the self-crowned saint of philanthropy. There was no evidence that her husband or anyone else existed. Yes, this was a temple dedicated to the modern-day supreme being of charitable giving, Tammy Crawford.

"Well, what do you think of my office?" Tammy asked when they were both seated, Tammy behind her desk.

Marty swallowed. "I think you've created a room that is perfect for your passion, philanthropy."

"Yes, I certainly have," Tammy simpered, a smug smile plastered across her face. "And now that Melissa Ross is dead, I am once again the reigning queen of Palm Springs philanthropy."

"I heard she was dead. In fact, someone even mentioned that she'd been murdered. Have you heard anything about that?" Marty asked innocently.

"I don't know, but I sure wouldn't be surprised if someone killed her. People of culture, like my husband, Lew, and me, don't like to see trailer trash like her come into a town and think they can become a part of society by using the money they won in a lottery, for heaven's sake. That is just so tawdry. I mean, I always knew she was just a ghetto girl, so I wouldn't be at all surprised if she was murdered. Some people have no class, and they just have to be punished for not minding their place."

"I saw her at the gala the other night. The way you two hugged after her donation was announced, I thought you were good friends," Marty said.

"Oh no." Tammy sucked in her cheeks. "Normally I wouldn't let someone like that attend one of our events. People like my husband have more class in their little fingers than she had in her whole body. Unfortunately, the chairman of the Board of Directors insisted that she be allowed to attend, and now I know why."

"Why is that, Tammy?"

"I'm sure she dangled her money in front of him. Probably told him she'd donate something if he let her in, and then she did. Pathetic, if you ask me."

"Did she have any family? I don't think I've heard of any," Marty commented casually."

"I read once she had an uncle and a brother, but she was estranged from both of them. I'm sure with her background, we're better off not knowing about them." Tammy focused on Marty. "Enough about that little nothing. What kind of donations have you come up with, dear? I can always use them."

"After the gala the other night, I had a thought. The people who attend these events are usually wealthy, and wealthy people often have things that need to be appraised for insurance purposes. I was thinking I could donate a couple of appraisals, say, two days each. That would make each of the donations, including my time, my research, and the preparation of the report, worth about $2,000 a day, $4,000 per donation. Naturally, if the appraisal went beyond two days, I would expect to be compensated at my usual rate, but I think it might appeal to people, particularly since they'd have to get an appraisal anyway and pay for it."

Tammy gasped in delight. "Marty, I think that's a wonderful idea. I'm sure my husband would have bid on an appraisal if it had been in the silent auction the other night. He's doing his every few year thing of crying the blues to me, telling me that business is horrible, we're going to go broke, and I have to stop giving so much to my charities. It's almost like he's blaming me for business being bad. I told him he could sell some of the things he inherited, but he always says no to that idea."

"I'm sorry to hear that. I'm sure that presents a problem for your philanthropy interests."

"It might have been if Miss Trailer Trash was still alive and giving big money, but now that she's dead, I can lower my giving limits, and I'll still be the number one philanthropist in Palm Springs. Isn't it wonderful when things just work out?" Tammy beamed.

Murder doesn't seem to be a way of things working out, Marty thought, *but then again, that could be a powerful motive for some people. You just never know about people.*

"Tammy, what's the next step in giving a donation? I've never done anything like this, so I'm at a loss."

"Well, I'm certainly not, because this is what I do, and if I say so myself, quite well. Now that Melissa's left us, guess that's a better thing to say than she was murdered, anyhow, I can now reclaim my rightful title of Number One Philanthropist in Palm Springs. I'll give you a couple of fancy gift certificates. Fill them out and when you're in the area, just drop them by the house. I don't want it to seem like I'm throwing you out, but Lew called a little while ago and asked me to meet him and a client of his for cocktails. He was pretty happy when he called, because he'd heard about Melissa and knew I wouldn't feel compelled to give as much as I have the last couple of years in order to retain my title."

Marty nodded as she stood up. "Please tell him hello for me."

"I will. I'm so glad he won't have to worry any more. I probably shouldn't say this, but Melissa's death certainly makes our life easier. Anyway, I'm glad you came by." Tammy opened her desk drawer and took out some papers, handing them across the desk to Marty. "Here are the gift certificates. Let me walk you to the front door."

After Marty put the gift certificates in the trunk of her car, she started driving towards the Palm Springs Antique Shoppe, her thoughts going a mile a minute. She couldn't wait to talk to Jeff.

CHAPTER FIFTEEN

Jeff was in his office at the police station when he placed a call to the Barstow, California police department. "This is Detective Jeff Combs with the Palm Springs Police Department. May I please speak with Chief Ellsworth?"

"I'll connect you," said the woman on the other end of the line.

A moment later, a familiar voice said, "Jeff, I haven't talked to you since the conference in Santa Barbara for Southern California police personnel, and that was almost a year ago. It's good to hear from you. I assume this isn't a social call, and that you're not down the street and want to meet me for a cup of coffee."

Jeff laughed and stretched back, putting his legs up on his desk. "Wish I could buy you that cup, but you're right, this isn't a social call. I'm calling about a man by the name of Christopher Ross. He lives on the outskirts of Barstow in one of those tarpaper shacks that your city is famous for having. I kind of have an address, but I don't know how valid it is."

"Often, not very, but it would help. Why are you interested in him?"

Jeff told him about Melissa's death, and that there was a good chance it was murder. He went on to tell him what he knew about

Melissa and her rags to riches story.

"I remember something about that," the chief said. "Think one of the secretaries here was talking about how this rich woman in Palm Springs had come from here. It had to do with her winning the Mega Millions. Think I may have even read the article."

"Well, here's the thing. The man I'm interested in is Melissa's uncle, but this is the clincher. She didn't know if he was alive or not, but she specifically disinherited him by name. I guess where I'm going with this is if she was murdered, and he thought he was an heir, maybe he even read that article, anyway, that could be a powerful motive. Naturally, he might become a person of interest. My favor is to ask if you could send one of your men out to where he lives and talk to him or even a neighbor, if he's not around. I don't know what I'm looking for, but anything would help. Here's what Melissa's attorney has as an address for him."

The chief listened and then said, "That's in a very poor area, Jeff. Most of the people who live out there either live off the grid or from disability check to disability check, but I'll have one of my guys see what he can find out. I assume you'd like this right away. Would I be right?"

Jeff laughed. "Don't think I even need to answer that, because if the conversation were reversed, you'd be asking the same."

"You got that right. I'll get back to you as soon as we come up with something. To change the subject, are you going to attend that conference in Los Angeles later this month? I've been thinking about attending it, but I'm getting pretty close to retirement, so I probably could pass on it."

"My police chief is going, so no need for me to go," Jeff said. "But I'll tell you what. I remember how much you liked that good wine from Sonoma we had at the conference. After I hear back from you, you might just have to sign for a package from me. How does that sound?"

"Good enough for me to get my man started on it today. Talk to you later," Chief Ellsworth said, ending the call.

*****

"Ricky, would you come to my office for a minute? Need you to do a little research for me," Jeff said into his phone.

"On my way, boss," the young detective said.

A few minutes later there was a knock on Jeff's door. "Come in," Jeff said, gesturing to him.

"You wanted to see me, boss?"

"Yes, Ricky. Sit down. This is regarding the Melissa Ross case. I've talked several times to her lawyer, and it turns out that Melissa had a brother by the name of Edward Ross. She told the lawyer she didn't know if he was still alive, because he ran away from the home where they both lived with their uncle after their parents died. She told the lawyer he'd become a gang member, and that was the last she knew about him. Melissa said she assumed he was dead or in prison. According to the lawyer, he'd insisted that she specifically disinherit him in both her trust and will."

"I wouldn't think that would make the brother very happy if he is alive. Hear she was bucks up," the younger man said.

"She was. She won the Mega Millions lottery some years ago, and it was one of the largest payouts ever. She was a very, very wealthy woman."

"If she disinherited him, why do we care about him?" Ricky looked confused.

"Detective Bryant, there's a good chance she was murdered. We're looking at anyone who might have a motive. I'd say a poor brother who had a rich sister and didn't know he'd been disinherited sure might make him a person of interest."

"Yeah, hadn't thought of it that way." The young detective rubbed his chin. "Guess he might have a motive. What do you need from me?"

"I want you to find him. All we have to go on is that he was with a gang. Over twenty years ago, there was a lot of gang activity in Bakersfield that spilled over into Barstow and surrounding towns. The big one was the East Side Victoria Gang. The local police authorities finally shut the door on that gang just a few years ago. There's a good chance that was the gang Ed Ross was involved in."

"I remember hearing about them when I was in the academy. Good thing it's no longer operating."

"Couldn't agree more. I think you need to start by doing a search of his name using the statewide criminal data base information and then go from there. If you find out he was incarcerated, get all the details, when, for how long, everything. If he's out, find out where he went. Put this on fast track. Since I'm the one who gives you your assignments, this takes precedence over everything else. Understand?"

Just then Jeff's phone rang and he picked it up. "Detective Combs."

"Detective, this is Darcourt LeBleu over at the coroner's office. Your sister-in-law left a little while ago. Nice lady. Don't know if she found out anything that will help on this case, but I wanted to let you know that I just received the preliminary finding on the cause of death. Quite frankly, this is a new one for me. Evidently Melissa Ross died from a poison dart frog secretion. That accounts for the puncture wound on her arm."

"Seriously, Darcourt, a poison dart frog secretion was the cause of death? That's something I know nothing about. Where does someone get stuff like that?"

"I have no idea. Like I said, this is a new one for me. I'm going to spend a little time researching it, but I thought I better alert you.

However, this is definitely a homicide. She was obviously killed by another person, which means you now officially have a murder investigation on your hands. Good luck trying to solve this one. It really has a strange twist to it."

"Thanks. I appreciate it. Think I better do some research as well," Jeff said before ending the call.

"Sir, I couldn't help but overhear about the poison dart frog," Ricky said. "I had to go on a mission a few years ago. Our church requires that young men spend two years on one, and we have no idea where we're going. We can't even request a favorite place where we want to go. I spent some time at the training center in Provo, Utah and then was sent to Costa Rica. I became pretty proficient in Spanish."

Jeff began to impatiently tap his pen on the desk. "Ricky, I fail to see what this has to do with a poison dart frog."

"I'm getting there, sir. Poison dart frogs come from South American and Central American countries. Remember the stories about natives using darts with something on them to kill their enemies? Well, what they used was the secretion from a poison dart frog. I actually went to a store in Costa Rica where people could buy them. The owner told me he had several people who smuggled them into the United States and mentioned that some city in California, he thought it was Palm Springs, had a guy who sold them. Being a native Californian, it kind of stuck with me."

"Obviously, you know a lot more about this than the coroner and I do. In addition to getting the information about Melissa's brother, see what you can find out about it. Particularly if there's someplace in Palm Springs where you can get one of these frogs."

"Yes, sir. I'll get right on it. Interesting case. I'll let you know as soon as I have anything." Ricky's chair scraped on the floor as he got up.

"Thanks." Before Ricky got to the door, Jeff was making notes, and deciding what needed to be done next. He wondered how Marty's appointments had gone and started to call her, but realized he'd be home in a couple of hours, and it could wait until then.

CHAPTER SIXTEEN

"Carl, I really appreciate you doing this for me. I owe you. Are you going to close the shop while we visit Mrs. Taylor?" Marty asked him.

"No, I have a young woman working for me now two afternoons a week. She wants to become an antique appraiser, and I'm helping her learn the trade. In return she comes here, dusts, moves things around, greets customers, and generally does what I ask. It's been great, because for the first time I can actually make appointments away from the shop without having to close it. It certainly has helped me financially."

Carl nodded towards a blond woman who was rearranging the window display.

"I give her the latitude to lower the prices a bit if she feels it's necessary on smaller items in order to sell them. You know, some people won't buy anything unless they feel they're getting a deal and unfortunately, this profession lends itself to that practice. You'd be amazed how much she sells while I'm gone. That's money that would have been spent somewhere else if my shop had been closed." He patted his hip pocket where the faint outline of his wallet could be seen. "So, I'm ready to go to our appointment, are you?"

"I am, and I'm looking forward to it for a number of reasons. We can take my car," Marty said.

"Good. You drive, and I'll direct you where to go. I won't be gone long, Megan," Carl said to the woman working on the window display as they made their way out.

A few minutes later he said, "It's just up ahead. See that big glass and wood house on the right? That's hers."

"Wow, it's beautiful," Marty said as she headed towards the house he was pointing to. "It's not exactly a desert style home, but it doesn't bounce like a Queen Ann house or some similar style would."

"Rhonda has very good taste. You'll see antiques and collectibles that museums would be happy to own. Let's do it," he said, opening his car door when they had pulled up in front of the house.

They walked up the tree-lined walkway with large expanses of grass on either side. "Rhonda told me once that one of the nice things about being rich was you could afford to give the grass all the water it needed, even if you do live in the desert."

"Carl, this seems awfully coincidental. Melissa and Tammy's homes are within a block of here and each of their homes is beautiful, very large, and yet totally different from the one another. I mean here are three wealthy women who could afford to buy about any house in Palm Springs, but each has chosen her own style."

"This part of old Palm Springs is definitely not like the McMansion variety of some of the newer golf course communities." He rang the bell and a moment later, a pretty young Spanish woman opened the door.

"*Buenos tardes*, Maylin. We have an appointment with Mrs. Taylor," Carl said.

"*Si*, please come in. I will get her," the maid said in a soft voice.

"I didn't know you spoke Spanish, Carl. I'm impressed," Marty said.

"Don't be. You've just heard about all the words I know. Obviously, not many."

"Maylin is quite beautiful. Her jet-black hair is so shiny, it's almost blue. And that gorgeous coffee-colored complexion. I'm envious."

"She's been with Rhonda for several years. She's from Costa Rica. Believe it or not, there are quite a few people from there who live in the Palm Springs area. I think it's called chain migration. You know, when people from one country come to the United States they tend to settle in communities where others from their country are living, which makes sense to me. If I went to a foreign country, I'd want to be with people from the United States. Think the term for that is ex-pat."

They stood in the airy hallway, waiting for their hostess. "So, does the fact you know about it suggest that you're thinking of moving?" Marty joked.

"Are you kidding? I've worked too hard to establish myself here, darling, and I have so many friends…"

They were interrupted by the arrival of an imposing auburn-haired woman, who appeared to be in her sixties, but with the amount of "help" she must have received from one or more plastic surgeons, it was hard to tell.

"Carl, it's so good to see you," the woman said flirtatiously. "And you must be Marty Morgan. Welcome to my home. Carl speaks very highly of you." Rhonda Taylor extended her hand to shake Marty's. "Let's go into the kitchen. Please, follow me. Before she left for the day, my cook, Lucille, prepared some lemonade and sugar cookies for us. I thought we could talk for a moment before I show you around."

"That would be lovely," Marty said. "Thank you for letting me come with Carl." While Rhonda was plating the cookies and pouring the lemonade into glasses, Marty looked closely at her.

Rhonda was quite tall, with a dancer's grace and poise. She wore

MURDER & MEGA MILLIONS

slim grey silk pants with a silver silk blouse. Her jewelry was understated, a silver necklace with a large diamond teardrop and silver and diamond earrings. She wore a silver cuff on her wrist which accentuated her white gold wedding band. Marty wished she could achieve the innate elegance that Rhonda carried off so easily, but figured that was something you were born with. You couldn't learn it.

"Here you are. Please, have a cookie and some lemonade. Carl, I'm just dying to show you what I got at the auction, although I have to admit that *nouveau riche* carpetbagger, Melissa Ross, got a couple of pieces I would have liked to own. Maybe there will be some kind of an estate sale, and I can get them then."

She frowned, and continued speaking. "I heard the news about her, and I can't say I'm sorry she's dead. Good riddance. It's a pity when someone comes to town and thinks big money gives them the right to take over what people have worked long and hard for."

"Rhonda, you know I understand your feelings about Melissa. I'm sure it's a relief to know that your position as the premier art and antique collector in Palm Springs is once again yours alone," Carl said.

"It certainly is, but then again there's something called karma. I guess it was karma, her death and all. Upstart deserved it. Anyway, let me take you on a tour. Please follow me."

For the next hour Rhonda walked them through each room showing off her impressive collections. Marty had to admit the woman had impeccable taste. Her art and antiques were some of the best Marty had ever seen. When they were getting ready to leave, the phone rang in Rhonda's office, and she excused herself to get it. She closed the door and answered it.

Laura and Jeff were always kidding Marty about the fact she could hear a pin drop when no one else could. She didn't know why, but she'd been blessed with an elevated sense of hearing, and she couldn't help but overhear the conversation Rhonda was having with her husband, Dr. Wesley Taylor.

"What do you mean you can't make it home and go to the dinner party with me? Don't tell me you have to work late. I know you're with your little tramp. I've been thinking, dear husband, I haven't seen you for three days. Maybe it's time something happened to that little tart of yours. If she wasn't around, you wouldn't need to spend all of your money on her, would you? I'm getting very tired of you putting me on a starvation budget. Do me a favor and tell the trollop she better watch her backside, because someone might want to help her have a bad accident. If that happened, I could have the money you're wastefully squandering on her."

Carl was oblivious to the conversation. He'd wandered into the living room, and was looking at the some of the pieces Rhonda had recently bought. Marty's heart was racing. She hadn't eavesdropped, but she'd just overheard a conversation that sounded extremely ominous. She knew she had to tell Jeff about it and see what could be done, if anything. From the threat Rhonda had just made, it seemed like Dr. Wesley's mistress might be in danger. Marty moved away from where she was standing in the hallway and joined Carl in the living room.

Evidently, based on what Marty had just heard, Rhonda Taylor had a side to her that few people knew about. Marty wondered if Melissa had seen that side of her. Who knows? It may have been the last thing Melissa saw.

A few moments later a smiling Rhonda walked down the hall to the living room where Carl and Marty were waiting for her. "I'm sorry about that. It was my husband telling me how much he misses me and that he'd be home soon. You wouldn't think a man would be so attentive after so many years of marriage. I must be the luckiest woman in the world. Thank you both for coming. I love to show off my treasures to people, and now that Melissa isn't around to take any away from me, I can have them all. Yes, life is very good."

Carl and Marty thanked her again, left the house, and got into Marty's car.

"Well, what did you think?" Carl asked.

Marty intentionally guarded her response. "I agree with what you said earlier. She has an incredible eye and incredible collections. Thanks again for setting it up."

"Did you find out anything that will help you or Jeff?" he asked, clearly wanting to get some tidbits of gossip from her so he could scatter them here and there.

"I'm not sure. I need to think about it." She knew if she told him about the phone conversation she'd overheard between Rhonda and her husband, it would be all over Palm Springs before morning. And she still wasn't sure what all of it meant.

She dropped Carl off at his shop and spent a lot of time thinking about what she'd heard as she drove back towards the compound in High Desert.

CHAPTER SEVENTEEN

Marty was having trouble trying to make sense of what she'd learned. She knew the two meetings she'd had could be important to Jeff's investigation. When she pulled into the driveway, Patron and Duke were waiting at the gate for her, bringing a smile to her face.

"Hi, guys," she said to the dogs as she unlatched the gate. "How was your afternoon?" She bent down to pet both of them. Duke wagged his tail, greeting her with a sloppy dog kiss on her hand. Patron sniffed her legs, and then backed up, growling with the guard hairs down the center of his back stiffened. He continued to growl until Laura came to the gate to see what the problem was. She knelt down and spoke softly to him, and a few minutes later he, too, wagged his tail and slobbered on Marty's hand.

"Laura, we need to talk about what's going on with him, but first let me take my things into the house. Back in a minute," she said as she waved to Jeff, Les, John, and Max, who were seated at the big picnic table in the courtyard. She walked into the house followed by Duke and Patron.

A few minutes later Marty walked out to the courtyard and after Jeff lightly kissed her he said, "Sit down, sweetheart. I've got some important news for you. The coroner has confirmed that Melissa was murdered. Whoever did it used some strange type of poison produced by a poison dart frog. I've already shared this information with the others here at the table, but I wanted you to know, too. So now I've got a full-blown murder case that I have to solve. We've been waiting to hear about your meetings, and I didn't want Laura to tell us about her meeting with the coroner until you were here."

"Wow," Marty said. "That's a real shocker, when you consider Melissa was so well-thought of here in the Palm Springs area. But before we start discussing our meetings, I have to ask Laura something. Laura, you briefly mentioned psychic dogs. Can you tell us anything else about them?"

"This is about Patron, isn't it?" Laura asked as she took a sip from her wine glass.

"Yes, I stopped by the Hi-Lo Drugstore this afternoon on my way into town. Lucy wanted to see a picture of the newest addition to the compound. It led to an interesting conversation. Here's what she said." Marty recounted to the group what Lucy had said about psychic dogs. When she was finished, the group collectively looked at Laura, curious as to what her response would be.

Laura was silent for several moments. When she finally spoke, her voice was quiet but firm. "I haven't wanted to say a lot about it, but ever since Patron acted strange before you went to the gala, I've been wondering just how extensive his psychic powers are. His behavior has been unusual." She looked at Marty. "Remember when he didn't want us to go to the appraisal and how he acted? When you got home this evening, it confirmed what I'd researched today."

"Laura, this is making me really nervous. Get to it," Marty said, while Jeff poured her a glass of wine.

"Okay. I found out that there are numerous instances of where dogs have had psychic abilities. I think I mentioned before that a lot of people with health issues such as epilepsy have therapy dogs, or I'd call them psychic dogs. These dogs know when their owner is about to have an epileptic seizure, and steps can be taken to prevent it or mitigate it. Also, there are a number of instances where a dog has diagnosed cancer," Laura said.

"Yes, but I wouldn't call those things psychic," John said. "Surely it's just what we call animal instinct, isn't it?"

"Well, think about it. At some level these dogs have sensed something from a paranormal perspective. In other words, what they have sensed is beyond the normal five senses of sight, smell, hearing, taste, and touch. I would call it using psychic abilities."

The other five were silent while they thought about what she'd just said, and then Jeff spoke up. "When you first mentioned it, I didn't take you too seriously, but let's say we agree with what you've just said. I assume you're saying that some dogs are capable of having a sixth sense and that Patron has that sense. Would I be right?"

"That's exactly what I'm saying. Patron is apparently able to sense things about Marty. For instance, the night of the gala Marty saw Melissa, who was murdered a few days later. I think the morning Marty and I discovered Melissa, Patron was in some sort of a psychic state. It seems to have something to do with warning Marty that there is danger."

"I can see why that might be," Marty said, "if we accept that Patron's psychic, but how do you explain his behavior when I got home this evening? He was agitated again, but I never saw Melissa today."

Laura continued in earnest. "When I got home after my meeting with the coroner, I did some research on dogs, specifically their psychic abilities regarding danger and death. There have been numerous instances where dogs have warned their owners before a disaster or danger. I feel pretty certain that Patron is metapsychically linked to you, Marty, and he's hard-wired to let you know when you're in danger."

"That would explain why you can calm him down. Kind of a one psychic to another type of thing, but that still doesn't explain the way he greeted me this evening," Marty said. "What do you make of that?"

Laura thought it over. "I think it has something to do with your meetings today. I think one of those women presents a danger to you, and in the only way he can, Patron is letting you know about it."

"I'll go along with everything you've said up to this point," Marty said. "But I fail to see how two of the most prominent women in Palm Springs present a threat to me."

"Keep thinking about it. I have no idea what or who it is, but Patron does," Laura said with finality.

"Okay, on that note, it's time for dinner," John said, "but from now on, I'm going to be looking over my shoulder at Patron. Anyway, dinner is kind of a feel-good thing we serve at the Pony. People love it, and I thought you could use something to make you feel better given what's been going on in the last couple of days. It's my take on a bacon and egg sandwich. After that, get ready for the dessert. It's pretty spectacular. Max and I will be serving you shortly."

After he'd finished his first sandwich, Les said, "You can serve this to me anytime. Actually, I'll take another one. I need the energy." John passed around the platter of the bacon and egg sandwiches and was pleased to note that everyone helped themselves to a second one. It was pretty apparent why the sandwich was such a hit at the Red Pony.

After they finished eating the sandwiches, John said, "At the receptions, cocktail parties, and other events that aren't sit down dinners, we pretty much serve finger food. Desserts are usually cookies or small pieces of cake or little tarts that can be eaten without utensils. Since almost everyone loves chocolate, I thought a chocolate platter or even a chocolate bar, depending on the client's available space, would be fun. Give me a minute, and I'll get my rendition of one." He and Max stood up and walked towards his kitchen.

When they returned, they were each carrying large white square platters with different kinds of chocolate candies and pieces of chocolate bars on them.

"John, this is beautiful," Marty said, looking over the delights before them. "You've got white chocolate, milk chocolate, dark chocolate, and truffles, and even some with nuts and caramel. I like the addition of chopped apples and dried fruit. Keeps the tongue from sticking to the roof of your mouth. Problem is, I don't know where to begin."

It was quiet in the compound as the residents slowly made their way through the chocolates.

"John, I'm sure I speak for everyone when I say that was a huge hit. Yes, you definitely need to serve this at your catering events. If you have the space, I'd set up a special table, maybe with roses or something kind of romantic. The only problem is, I ate so much chocolate, with all of the caffeine it has in it, I may never get to sleep," Les said, "but maybe that's okay. I've been working on a painting all day that I was hoping to finish, but didn't. The caffeine in the chocolate just might make me stay awake to do the last few things that need to be tweaked on it."

Les was one of the most well-known artists on the West Coast. His pieces commanded huge prices and each one sold as soon as the paint was dry on it. The San Francisco gallery that was his primary venue had a waiting list for them. He could easily afford to live anywhere in the world, but he'd grown to love the compound and the peace and quiet of the high desert. The fact he and Laura were devoted to each other was probably another factor.

"Laura, we'd all like to hear what happened at the coroner's today," Jeff said. "You're on."

CHAPTER EIGHTEEN

Max and John cleared the little that was left of the chocolate dessert trays and sat down, ready to hear about Laura's meeting with the coroner.

"This was a first for me," Laura began. "I met the coroner, Darcourt LeBleu, at the county morgue. He couldn't have been more gracious to me. We talked for a while about New Orleans and his background. He's Creole, and all I can say is that we sort of connected on some level. I think he has some psychic gifts he doesn't talk about. Anyway, I asked him if I could be alone with Melissa's body for a few minutes."

"Did ya' have the jimjams?" Max asked. "Know I would, bein' with a dead body. Jes' the thought of it gives me the icks." He wriggled his upper body about and made an ugly face.

"No, I didn't feel that way. Here's what happened. Darcourt had put her body on a table in a cold room in the morgue. He left me alone with the body and closed the door. I immediately felt something, but I didn't know what it was. A shimmering light started to hover over her body, and then it turned into what I guess you'd call a female ghost."

There was an audible sound of breaths being drawn in as the five others at the table leaned forward so they wouldn't miss a word of what Laura was saying.

"This ghost, or apparition, or whatever you want to call it, seemed to be very kind. I decided to treat it as a real person, so I asked who she was. She told me, or I sensed it, or her response entered me by osmosis. I just don't know how it happened, but in one way or another she was able to communicate with me. Anyway, she said she was Melissa's mother, just as I told you I'd suspected. I asked her if she knew anything about Melissa's murder, such as who the murderer was." Laura paused and took a sip from the glass of water in front of her.

"Well, what did she say?" John asked, hanging on every word she said.

"She told me she got there too late to save her daughter, but she saw someone running out of the house, and she had a feeling it was a woman. She said ever since she herself had died, she'd been able to protect Melissa, but this time it was too late. She said the only blessing was that Melissa had died almost instantly and she was glad whoever it was had used frog poison…"

Jeff interrupted her. "Wait a minute. Did she specifically used the term 'frog poison'?"

"Yes." Laura nodded vigorously. "At the time I had no idea what she meant by that. But now it makes sense to me since the coroner told you that Melissa's death was caused by poison produced by a poison dart frog. Do you know anything about it?"

"Very little, but here's the interesting thing." Jeff said. "One of the detectives working on the case was in my office when Darcourt called. Like I told you earlier, Darcourt told me the preliminary cause of death was attributed to the secretion from a poison dart frog. The detective who was there overheard the conversation. Turns out he knew about these types of frogs from the time he spent in Costa Rica, one of the countries where they are found. He's looking into it for me."

"I don't know how that fits in with what Melissa's mother said about it, but that's way too much of a coincidence," Laura said. "Anyway, the apparition told me she had to leave because very soon she and Melissa would be together again. Then she disappeared."

"That was it?" Jeff asked.

"Yes. I waited a few more minutes to see if she'd return. I know you're going to say this is pretty weird, but I'd swear I saw something leave Melissa's body. Maybe it was her spirit, and she and her mother are together again. That's just speculation on my part, but who am I to say that's not what happened?"

Everyone sitting at the table was quiet, then Laura spoke again. "I know how difficult this must be for all of you to believe, but it's the truth, just the way I described it." She turned to Jeff and said, "Does this help you at all?"

"At the moment, no. If it was a woman, as this ghost image of yours implied, that rules out Melissa's brother and uncle. I find the frog poison reference really interesting, and I'll be curious to see what my guy comes up with. He said he visited a place in Costa Rica that sold poison dart frogs, and he was told they are commonly smuggled into the United States, particularly California."

He turned to Marty and said, "Marty, you met with two women today. Since Laura's ghost indicated a woman did it, maybe one of them is the murderer. Although I find it hard to believe either one of those two pillars of society would have been involved in Melissa's murder."

"So do I, but my meetings were interesting. Both of those women hated Melissa for taking over their respective spots as number one, either in philanthropy or art and antiques. I did hear things from them, however, that might make either of them a suspect. Let me recap what I found out." She told them about both of her meetings and how happy each of them had been that Melissa was no longer around.

When she finished, Jeff said, "Even if one of them was the killer, the only shred of evidence I have is that Laura heard a ghost say that she thought it might have been a woman. Plus, there's nothing I can think of that would tie either one of them to a poison dart frog. Trust me, those are not grounds for arrest. If I arrested one of them based on what we have so far, I'd end up looking like a fool and my days as a detective would be long gone."

Jeff let out a sigh. "Ladies, I appreciate what you did today, but I have to say I'm not much further along in this investigation than I was last night. I guess now I need to look for a frog and a ghost. These are things I was never taught at the academy."

By mutual consent, the six of them headed for their respective homes. Max stayed overnight at John's, since they were catering an early morning breakfast. After Jeff had walked the dogs, and he and Marty were turning off the lights, he looked over at Patron and said to her, "What if Laura's right?"

"About what?" Marty asked, her hand on the bathroom door.

"What if Patron sensed you were in danger today because of your meetings with Tammy and Rhonda. What if Laura's ghost was right, and it was a woman?"

"Still won't stand up in court, Detective," she said with a knowing look and a shake of her head.

"I know, but Laura sure has proven to be right in the past when she helped us with other murder investigations."

"Whatever it is, it will wait until tomorrow. Get a good night's sleep, and maybe something will come to you in a dream."

"'Fraid not, sweetheart, I missed out on getting the psychic gene. I'm going to have to solve this the old school way, but I sure am anxious to find out what my detective finds out about the poison dart frog."

CHAPTER NINETEEN

The following morning Marty leaned over, kissed Jeff, and said, "Sorry to tell you this, Detective, but it's time to get up. I'm sure you have a busy day and I start the Ross appraisal today. I'll take the dogs out."

His answer was an unintelligible grunt.

When she'd finished letting the dogs commune with nature, she made coffee, sliced some bagels and tomatoes, and took honey mustard, an avocado, and smoked salmon out of the refrigerator. She loaded the various different toppings on a large breakfast tray and placed it on the kitchen table, then walked down the hall to the bathroom, a coffee cup in each hand.

"Thanks, sweetheart," Jeff said, grabbing one of the cups from her and taking a gulp. "I need this since my caffeine level has gone down to zero. I'm kind of like a car that needs gas, only in my case it's the caffeine I get from a cup of strong, black coffee. Marty, I really need to get a handle on this case. The chief has been bugging me because Melissa Ross was sort of a celebrity, and a celebrity's murder has to be solved quickly or the natives get restless."

"Seems like kind of a cold calculated approach. I would think all murders should get the same degree of attention from the police department."

"In a perfect world, Marty, they would, but the world isn't perfect. I didn't make the rules, but if I want to keep my job, I darn well better play by them." He put the cup down and smoothed his short sideburns in the mirror.

"Okay, I get your point. Your breakfast is on the kitchen table. The only thing you need to do is toast your bagel and then top it off with whatever looks good to you."

"I'm on it. I'll be leaving as soon as I finish eating. Actually, I might just take it with me. I really do need to get to my office, so have a good day, and check in with me if you discover anything I should know about while you're on your appraisal, and I'll see you tonight."

Marty took her coffee into the bedroom and got ready to go to the Ross home, making sure she had all of her appraisal equipment. She got the dogs organized for the day and knocked on Laura's door. When Laura opened it she said to Marty, "I gather by the photo bag on your shoulder and the big tote, that you're on your way to the appraisal. Right?"

"Yes. I'm going to be gone most of the day. I slipped a note under Les' door, asking him if he'd kind of watch over the dogs, although they have a doggie door so they can get out to the courtyard. But I'd just like someone to be on the lookout in case there's a problem. Since he said he was going to work on a painting after we finished dinner last night, I figured he was probably awake most of the night, so I don't want to bother him right now. I'm sure he's sleeping in."

"No problem. I'll check in with him later," Laura said as she tried to stifle a yawn. "I know he loves the dogs, so I'm sure he won't mind. I'll be curious if you find out anything when you're at the Ross home. Give me a call if you need me."

"Will do, and thanks!"

As she walked towards her car, Patron, who was standing in front of the gate, started growling as if he was telling Marty he was not letting her go to Melissa's home. For several minutes, Marty tried unsuccessfully to get him to move, but to no avail. Finally, she retraced her steps to Laura's house and knocked on the door again.

"Thought you were leaving," Laura said.

"I did too, but it looks like Patron has other plans for me, since he won't let me out the gate, and he's growling. I really need to get to that appraisal. Could you do your woo-woo stuff and calm him down enough so I can leave?"

"Let me see what I can do," Laura said, following Marty out to the front gate. She knelt down and spoke softly to Patron for several minutes, then she stood up. "Okay, I think he's calmed down enough that you can leave. I'm certain this has to do with the Ross murder. I have a feeling you'll know more later."

"Thanks, Sis," Marty said as she quickly opened the gate and walked to her car. She glanced back and saw that Patron and Duke were on their bellies behind the gate, in their usual places, ready and waiting for Marty to return.

CHAPTER TWENTY

When Jeff got to his office the red light on the phone was blinking, indicating he had a message. He pressed the button to retrieve his voicemail. "Good morning, Jeff. This is Chief Ellsworth. I have some information regarding Christopher Ross that I think you'll be interested in. Give me a call when you get a chance."

While he was on the phone, his secretary, Luisa, brought him a cup of coffee, something she did each morning. She knew that her boss worked much better when his coffee cup was full. Instead of returning to her desk, she stayed in his office until he'd finished listening to the message.

"Sir, you might want to go into the men's room and wipe off whatever it is you spilled on your shirt. Probably wouldn't look too professional if the other detectives that work for you see it."

Jeff glanced down at his shirt and saw the yellow stain she was referring to. "Thanks, Luisa. I ate breakfast on the way here. It's probably some honey mustard. I appreciate it." He followed her out of his office and went to the men's room and dabbed the spill off of his shirt with a paper towel.

Honey mustard was the bad boy, he thought, *but it sure was good. Well worth the spill. Wish I'd brought two of those bagels in the car with me, rather than just one.*

When he got back to his office he called Chief Ellsworth on his personal line. "That was fast," the chief said.

"Obviously, I got your message. What did you find out?"

"I sent one of my new men out to where this guy Ross lives. He said it really was a tarpaper shack. There's a lot of them in that area. The people who live out there aren't even the working poor. They're just poor."

"Yeah, I remember thinking when I drove through Barstow several years ago the city certainly was no stranger to an impoverished population. Actually, to be socially correct, I suppose I should use the term 'economically disadvantaged' rather than saying just plain old 'dirt poor.' Anyway, you know what I mean."

"True, but fortunately, we don't have a lot of crime problems out there," the chief said. "Our problems are more gang-related in the city. Anyway, here's what my guy got. He went up to the shack's door, or what would barely pass for being a door, and knocked. No one came to the door. There was a rusted old truck parked next to the shack, so he assumed someone was there. He walked around to the side of the shack and looked in a window. A man was asleep on the couch, although from the number of empty beer cans scattered around on the floor next to the couch, my guy assumed he was passed out. No amount of knocking on the door roused him."

Jeff thought for a few seconds. "Well, that accounts for yesterday, but that doesn't clear him on the day of the murder."

"I'm getting to that. My guy talked to a couple of Ross' neighbors. They verified that Mr. Ross had left his shack a couple of times for about a half an hour. They said that was his normal behavior. Evidently, when he ran out of beer, he'd go to the nearby gas station that had a convenience store and get more."

Jeff scribbled down some notes on the pad on his desk as the chief continued speaking. "They said he hadn't been gone from the shack for as long as either of them could remember for more than a half an hour on any given day. That would include the day that Melissa Ross was murdered. I think that effectively takes him off of the viable suspects list, because there is no way he could have made a round trip to Palm Springs and back in half an hour. He couldn't even drive to Palm Springs in that amount of time. Hope that helps."

"It does. As you well know, eliminating a suspect is an important part of solving a crime, but I just wish I had a viable suspect about now. Thanks, I really appreciate it."

"Think you got that wrong, Jeff. I'll be the appreciating one when I get a notice from FedEx that an adult must be home to sign for that wine you're going to be sending me." The chief let out a chuckle. "Here's my home address, and if you need anything else, happy to help." He gave Jeff his street name, the number, and his zip code. When he'd finished, he ended the call.

Well, one down, Jeff thought. *That leaves the brother as the only viable suspect. Swell. I'm not seeing any ties to either of the women Laura talked about. This is really frustrating.* He was staring into space, thinking about what to do next when his phone rang.

"Sir, this is Ricky. If you have a minute, I'd like to tell you what I've found out about the victim's brother and the poison dart frog."

"Now would be a good time. Come to my office."

*****

"Have a seat, Ricky. Care for a cup of coffee?"

"No thanks sir, I don't drink it." Ricky sat across from Jeff on the opposite side of his desk.

Jeff got straight to the point. "Okay, what have you found out?"
"First let me tell you about Ed Ross, the victim's brother. He was a member of the East Side Victoria gang. It looks like he was the fall guy for a drug deal that went really bad. The rest of the gang members got away, but he was arrested and sentenced to twenty-five

years in Kern Valley State Prison. He got out last week, which I think would make him a likely suspect. But here's the thing. He was diagnosed with Valley Fever the day before he got out of prison, and it was pretty much a death sentence."

Jeff exhaled. "I've heard of a lot of people in that area getting Valley Fever. I've read it comes from something in the soil, and with the wind they get over there in the San Joaquin Valley, it travels fast."

"That goes with what I found out."

"So, he got out of prison," Jeff said. "Since he probably didn't have any money other than what the state gave him when he got out, and he was ill, were you able to find out where he went?"

"Yes. I was pretty sure he didn't have much money, so I didn't bother checking airline manifests, instead I checked the buses." Ricky glanced down at his notebook. "I figured he'd probably taken one out of Delano. He did."

"And rode it to Palm Springs. Right?"

"Yes, sir. I found out he rented a room at a real flea bag of a motel, although I didn't find that out from any motel or hotel list."

"All right, Ricky. I'll bite." Jeff was intrigued. "How did you find that out?"

"Have no idea why I did what I did, but I checked with the coroner's office to see if they'd had any deaths recently from Valley Fever. I was told a maid at a motel had discovered a male body in one of the rooms when she went to clean it. The coroner's office determined that he'd died from Valley Fever. The identification they found in the room indicated the deceased individual was Ed Ross."

"Ricky, were you able to get the exact date of his death?"

"Yes, sir. He died the day before Melissa Ross did. He was in the cooler at the county morgue when she was murdered." The young detective sat back, clearly pleased by what he'd been able to find out.

Jeff was quiet for several moments and then said, "Well, that's the second suspect we can take off the possible suspects list. I was able to eliminate her uncle from what the Barstow police found out. This really puts me back to square one."

"Maybe not, sir. I did some research and found out some things about the poison dart frog I think you'll be interested in."

"I'm all ears. What did you find out?"

"I told you that I spent a lot of time in Costa Rica and even visited a store where they had poison dart frogs for sale. I think I also told you the man at the store said they smuggled a lot of them into the United States, particularly California, and that Palm Springs was often a destination point."

"Yes, Ricky, I remember. Go on."

"I speak Spanish pretty well, so I went to an area just outside of Palm Springs where a lot of Costa Ricans live. Seems like the whole neighborhood is made up of people that used to live in Costa Rica. For some reason, they've gotten a real stronghold in the gardening industry here. You know, all those golf courses have to be manicured by somebody, and a lot of them do that."

"Yes, I've seen a lot of Hispanics working on the golf courses as gardeners, but I didn't know they were Costa Rican."

"They are. Anyway, I got to talking to some of them and mentioned the poison dart frog. I asked them if they knew anyone who had them. I told them I had a friend who collected strange animals, and I thought he might enjoy having one. Several of them said the only person they knew who had them was a man by the name of Hector Diaz. One of them laughed and said 'You don't want to know how he gets them.' I laughed with them and told them I wouldn't ask."

Jeff leaned towards him. "Did you find him?"

"Yes. One of the men gave me directions to his ranch, if you want to call a couple of acres of dirt and a few shallow man-made ponds a ranch. There was a tiny little house on the property and that was it. About the only other things on the property were the ponds with bunches of leaves around them and some rain bird sprinklers. What was kind of surreal was that netting had been placed over the ponds the and surrounding leafy areas. It was actually pretty weird."

"It sounds like it. What was he like?"

"He was a nice guy," Ricky said, glancing down at his notebook again. "I'd say he was in his fifties. I told him I was interested in buying one of his frogs and told him the same story I'd told the people who referred me to him, namely, that I had a friend who collected strange animals. He took me out to one of the ponds covered with netting, and there must have been fifty frogs in it. They really are colorful. I saw blue ones, orange ones, yellow ones, and just about every other color in the rainbow."

Jeff was getting impatient. "Ricky, this is interesting, but I'm just not seeing a nexus to the Ross murder."

"I think there may be a link, and here's why. Hector's cell phone rang while we were out in the pond area, and he answered it. He talked to who I'm assuming was his niece, because he kept using the word, "*sabrino*," which is Spanish for niece. They were talking about a family member's upcoming *quinceanera*, you know, that big party they have when a girl turns 15. When they were finished with that, he started to say good-bye, and then he thanked her for sending her employer to him. He told her he was very happy because all the woman wanted was the secretion from the glands of the frog, and he could keep the frog. He told her the woman had paid him well."

"Were you able to find out who the woman was?" Jeff asked in anticipation.

"Yes. When he ended the call, he apologized to me and said that his niece worked for a very wealthy woman who was known throughout the Palm Springs area for her valuable collections of art and antiques. He said that his niece often talked about the beautiful things that were in the home where she worked as a maid five days a week."

Jeff had been making notes. He stopped and looked up hopefully. "Tell me you got the name of the woman, and you'll make the bad day I'm having look a lot better."

Ricky smiled. "I did. I said I knew a lot of people who were art and antique collectors, and I wondered if she was one of the people I know. He said her name was Rhonda Taylor. I looked her up and she's married to some bucks up doctor who has a little honey on the side. I hope that helps."

"More than you know, Ricky, more than you know, but I just don't quite know how I'm going to get from 'A' to 'B'. Nice job. I'll take it from here, although I'm not real sure where I'm going to take it. Don't know if I'll need it, but did you get the name of Mrs. Taylor's maid?"

"No, sir. I thought it might look like I was asking too many questions, but from the way he was talking, I got the impression that she was the only maid, as opposed to being one of several maids. If she's the only one who works for Mrs. Taylor, it shouldn't be too hard to find out her name."

"Great work, Ricky. I really appreciate how much you were able to find out in a short time. I may need your Spanish speaking abilities later on, depending on where this goes."

"You know where to find me, sir," Ricky said as he made his way out of Jeff's office.

CHAPTER TWENTY-ONE

When Marty arrived at the end of the Ross driveway, Isabella was waiting for her. Marty motioned for her to get in the car. "Good morning, Isabella, how are you today?"

"I am well, thank you," Isabella said and looked out the window as Marty drove up the long driveway and parked her car near the entryway.

"Here are your keys. I understand you'll be continuing to work here until the house is sold. If I have any questions regarding Miss Ross' art or antiques, I'm hoping you can help me."

"I will try." Isabella took the keys and opened the passenger side car door.

This must be very hard for her, Marty thought. *Hopefully, once she's in the house, she'll feel better. Anticipating something can often be worse than the real thing.*

A moment later they walked into the house. "I think I'll start in the dining room and do one room at a time. That seems like the simplest way to handle this," Marty said as she took the heavy camera off her shoulder and put it and her tote bag on the floor. For the next three hours she measured, dictated, and took photographs of Melissa's collections.

At noon she walked into the kitchen and said, "Isabella, I wasn't sure if there would be any food here, so I brought my lunch. I have plenty if you'd like to share it." Isabella had her back to Marty and silently shook her head. It became apparent that the young woman was avoiding her, and Marty had no idea why.

She decided the best way to find out why was to ask. "Isabella, I can see that you're upset. I'm sure this is a difficult time for you. May I help?"

Isabella turned around, and Marty saw the tears in her eyes. "No. It is something I will have to live with."

"I don't know what you mean, Isabella." Marty pressed her. "What will you have to live with?"

Isabella started sobbing. "I never should have come back and hidden in the kitchen. This is all my fault. If I'd just been stronger. I can't take this any longer, no matter what Tomas says."

Marty steered Isabella over to the table. "Sit down, Isabella, and start at the beginning. I have no idea who Tomas is. Tell me what's bothering you. Maybe I can help."

"No, there is no way you can help. I won't even be able to go to confession any more. I have sinned." Isabella sat down in a chair, sobbing uncontrollably, while Marty looked around for a tissue to give her. She found some in the small bathroom off the kitchen and handed them to Isabella, as she pulled out a chair and sat down next to her.

"What happened, Isabella? Why won't you be able to go to confession? How did you sin?"

Isabella dabbed her cheeks with the tissue. "After the auction the other night, I agreed to let Tomas come to the house and steal some of Miss Ross' art and antiques. He came up with a plan to sell her antiques so we could get enough money to get married. He was going to take a few items from the house and sell them in Los Angeles. I was to come here and hide in the kitchen while she was at the auction. When she came home, we thought she'd be happy, maybe even a little tipsy after her buys at the auction. When she went to her bedroom to go to bed, I was to call Tomas and tell him the coast was clear so he could come to the house, and I'd let him in." She started crying again and raised the balled-up tissue to her eyes.

"Did you call him?" Marty asked.

"Yes, but it didn't matter, because by the time I called him the woman had killed her. He never came to the house. Instead I ran out the back door and met him down the street where his truck was parked."

"Wait a minute, Isabella. I'm confused. You're saying Tomas was going to come here, but he didn't because you called him and told him Miss Ross was dead, is that right? You said a woman had killed her. How do you know it was a woman?"

"I saw her." Isabella looked wide-eyed at Marty.

"You saw the person who murdered Melissa Ross?" Marty asked incredulously.

"*Si, si.* I was stooping down behind the kitchen counter trying to hide when Miss Ross came into the house. Her driver helped her bring in some small items she'd bought at the auction. He left and she made several trips, taking them into her office. She always wrote down information about what she'd bought, like when, what it was, the price she paid, and anything else that was important, but she didn't do it that night. I guess she thought she'd do it the next day."

"She never came into the kitchen and discovered you?"

"No. It looked like she was just getting ready to go to her bedroom. In fact, she'd turned off several lights when there was a knock on the door. I was curious as to who would be visiting her at that time of night, so I peeked over the counter. Her back was to me when she answered the door. She must have known who the woman was, because she let her in, and they walked towards the living room." Isabella wiped tears from her eyes.

"Does that mean that you didn't recognize her?" Marty asked.

"*Si, si.* I have never seen her before. She was very beautiful. Tall, with auburn hair. Very, how do you say, elegant. Even though she was an older woman, she looked like maybe she'd been a model."

"All right. Let me get this straight. What happened when the woman came in?"

"Miss Ross seemed surprised to see her and told the woman she hoped there were no hard feelings because Miss Ross had the winning bid on several items the woman had wanted to buy at the auction they'd just been to." She started sobbing again and hung her head, clearly troubled and emotionally upset over what she had seen.

Marty rubbed her back. "What happened then, Isabella?"

"The woman said she had no hard feelings, and that she'd just stopped by to congratulate Miss Ross on successfully bidding on some very good pieces. And then, and then..." A hiccup escaped from Isabella's mouth.

"What happened then, Isabella?"

Isabella looked up at Marty. "She put her arms around Miss Ross for a moment, like she wanted to make up, kind of hugging her, and then Miss Ross fell to the floor. The woman pulled some kind of a needle out of Miss Ross' arm, you know, the kind drug addicts use, closed the living room doors, and left the house."

"If they were in the living room, how did you see her from the kitchen?" Marty asked.

"Is very easy. From here you can see a little into the living room."

Marty glanced through the doorway and from where she was

sitting saw that Isabella was telling the truth. The entrance to the living room was visible from their vantage point.

Marty racked her brain trying to remember something Jeff had said about the person who killed Melissa. She thought he said the killer had been very careful. She struggled to remember the context of what he'd said. Suddenly it came to her. It was something about there being no fingerprints.

"Isabella, did you notice if the woman pulled the living room doors closed with her hand?"

"Let me think." The maid was silent for several moments and when she spoke, she was no longer crying. "I remember now, because I thought it was very strange. She unwound the scarf she was wearing around her neck, covered one of her hands with it, and then pulled the doors closed using the hand covered by her scarf."

"Isabella, you said you didn't know the woman, but would you recognize her if you saw her or a picture of her?"

"*Si, si*. I will never forget what she looked like."

Marty gently brushed away a strand of Isabella's long black hair that had stuck to the young woman's wet cheek. "Isabella, you are not to blame for this. All you did was consent to being part of a burglary that never happened. There is nothing to blame yourself for, but I'm curious why you would agree to be an accessory to a robbery when you obviously cared so much for Miss Ross."

"It was Tomas. We're getting married, and he said we needed the money or we couldn't get married. I was afraid he would hurt me if I said no."

Marty saw Isabella's hands tremble in her lap. "Isabella, you had nothing to do with Melissa's murder, but there is something you need to do, and that's leave this Tomas man. You must not get married to a man you're afraid of, and no woman should be so afraid of a man she'd agree to be part of a felony. I know people who can help you."

"No, no," Isabella said, biting her lip. "If I leave Tomas he will find me, and he will hurt me. I know it."

Marty tried to reassure her. "I promise you he will not find you. My husband is a detective with the Palm Springs Police Department and they have a number of programs that provide help for women like you. Believe me, you are not alone. I'll call him now and tell him what you've told me."

She watched Isabella, who was staring at her in disbelief, obviously petrified. "Isabella, please believe me when I tell you that your life will be much better without Tomas. If you married him, you'd probably end up being a tragic statistic, like so many other women have been. You have done absolutely nothing wrong, and you deserve much better than to spend your life with a man you live in fear of."

Marty took her phone out of her purse and called Jeff while Isabella began to cry again, softly. "Jeff, it's me. I have some information about the Ross murder that you need to hear right away.

CHAPTER TWENTY-TWO

"Detective Combs, there's a man in the reception area who says he needs to speak to someone about the Ross murder. Since this is your case, I thought you'd probably want to talk to him. Shall I send him in?" Jeff's secretary, Luisa said, as she peered around the door.

Jeff looked up and nodded. "Yes, thank you. Did he say anything else?"

"No, just that he needed to speak to someone about the case."

"Did he give you his name?" Jeff asked.

"Yes, his name is Dr. Wes Taylor," she said as she walked out of his office.

Wes Taylor? That must be Rhonda Taylor's husband, he thought. *Weird. I wonder why he wants to see me.*

A few moments later, an attractive grey-haired man appeared in his doorway. Jeff stood up as the man entered his office. "You must be Dr. Taylor. Please, come in and have a seat," he said, gesturing to the chair on the other side of his desk. "How can I help you?"

When Dr. Taylor was seated, he stared gravely at Jeff. "Detective, I'm married to Rhonda Taylor, but quite frankly, it's been a marriage in name only for many years. My wife became consumed with buying art and antiques some years ago. I mean, really consumed. She's spent a small fortune on them. I'm not particularly proud of it, but over the years, I found companionship with various other women, if you know what I mean. In the past, Rhonda has always looked the other way."

"I'm getting the impression that the situation has recently come to a head." Jeff said, twirling a pen in his fingers as he looked at the man across from his desk. He was clearly troubled and from the dark circles under his eyes, it looked like he hadn't slept at all the previous night.

"It did. Several months ago, I told Rhonda that she would have to curb her spending, because my medical practice was less profitable than it had been in the past. Actually, between us, that wasn't true. I have fallen in love with a woman who makes me feel like I did when I first married Rhonda. Her name is Sylvia. I bought a condominium for her and am supporting her. I wanted to see how it worked out before I asked Rhonda for a divorce, but she beat me to it."

"She asked you for a divorce?" Jeff asked.

"No. I called yesterday afternoon to tell her I wouldn't be home last night and I was unable to go with her to a dinner party we'd been invited to attend. She was furious. She told me she knew all about where I was spending my money and my lady friend better watch her backside," Dr. Taylor said as he wrung his hands together. "I'm afraid, really afraid, that Rhonda will do something to harm her."

"Has your wife ever threatened to harm any other lady friends that you may have had in the past?"

"No, but something's happened to Rhonda in the last year or so. Prior to that, she'd established a reputation for herself as being the foremost collector of art and antiques in Palm Springs. The woman who was recently murdered, Melissa Ross, had usurped Rhonda's place. All she talked about, when we were together, which wasn't all that much, was how somebody should do something to Melissa Ross.

She vehemently felt that someone who won a lottery and started collecting art and antiques had no right to take over her place. I know it sounds nuts, but she really valued her status, and Miss Ross was clearly overshadowing her."

Not for the first time, Jeff was struck by the meaningless problems the rich often preoccupied themselves with. "Since Rhonda threatened your lady friend," he said, "are you saying you believe Rhonda may have had something to do with the death of Melissa Ross?"

"I wouldn't put it past her. The woman she is now is not the same woman I married. Something has happened to her. Quite frankly, as a psychiatrist, I've seen many people over the years who slip over the edge and become insane. I guess it's kind of like the shoemaker's children who don't have shoes. I missed the signs in my own wife." Dr. Taylor let out a resigned sigh. "Yes, Detective Combs, I definitely think Rhonda is capable of murdering someone, and I would not be the least bit surprised if she killed Melissa Ross. I just don't want her to kill Sylvia."

Jeff sat back in his chair, thinking about what his next step should be. He had some circumstantial evidence on Rhonda. Her husband thought she was insane and according to Ricky, a man who raised poison dart frogs said she'd bought something poisonous from him. The fact that Melissa had been murdered by a secretion from a poison dart frog also led to her being the leading suspect in the murder. What troubled Jeff was that's all he had, circumstantial evidence. There were no eyewitnesses.

While he was thinking about his options, his cell phone rang. He took it out of his pocket and saw that it was Marty. "Hi, sweetheart. I'm in a meeting. Can I call you back?" He listened to her and said, "Tell me everything. You're sure you're with someone who can identify the murderer?"

"Yes," Marty said, going back over the conversation she'd just had with Isabella.

"Meet me at the police station in about half an hour and bring this Isabella woman with you. I'll meet you there. I'm going to leave the station immediately and arrest Rhonda Taylor. We have enough to arrest her and bring her in, but not enough to take her to trial. I'm hoping your person can put the nail in her coffin, so to speak. Tell your person she won't be in the room with the woman she saw. She'll be in a separate room with a one-way window, and you'll be with her. See you then."

He ended the call and looked across at Wes Taylor, who was observing him in silence. "Dr. Taylor, you probably overheard that. I've decided to arrest your wife for the murder of Melissa Ross. I'm going to get a couple of my detectives and go over to your house. We'll bring her back here and see if the person I just learned about, who says she was a witness to the murder, can ID your wife. I'm going to want a statement from you as well regarding the threats she's made, so why don't you leave for now and come back here to the station in about an hour?"

"Detective, if my wife thinks I have anything to do with this, she'll go berserk. Do I have to confront her?"

"No. You'll be in a separate room, and she won't be able to see you. I'll see you in an hour," Jeff said, showing the doctor out.

He called Ricky. "Ricky, I want you to come to my office now. Get one of the other detectives as well. We're going to make an arrest in the Melissa Ross murder case."

CHAPTER TWENTY-THREE

"Isabella, we're going to the police station in about half an hour," Marty said gently. "My husband is going to arrest a woman for murdering Melissa Ross, but he needs you to identify her and see if it's the same person you saw. He said to tell you that she will never know you are there. You and I will be in a room with a one-way window in it. You'll be able to see the woman, but she won't be able to see you. You'll be completely safe, do you understand?"

Isabella started to say something, but Marty held her hand up as she picked up her ringing phone, indicating she had to take the call. She looked down at the monitor and saw that it was Les.

That's strange, she thought. *I don't think he's ever called me before. I hope nothing's wrong with the dogs.*

"Hi, Les. What's up?"

"I'm sorry to bother you, Marty, but Patron has gone completely nuts. He's growling and barking, and he's even rubbed some of his fur off, frantically trying to get the gate open. I called Laura, and she seemed to think he sensed something was going on with you. She told me to call you and see if there was, and if so, I should bring Patron to you, and she would meet us. She's pretty sure he needs to be with you, and since she seems to have a connection with him, she wanted to meet me if I took him to you."

"This is surreal, Les. Yes, I just got off the phone with Jeff, and I'm getting ready to meet him at the police station in half an hour. I'm taking a woman with me who says she saw the person who murdered Melissa Ross. Jeff will be arresting her momentarily."

"In that case, Patron and I will meet you at the police station. I'll call Laura and tell her to meet us there as well. I just hope he calms down enough that I can drive with him in my car."

"Les, I have a wire mesh screen in the garage I've used before for the dogs when I've gone somewhere with them and didn't want them to get in the front seat. It should fit in your SUV perfectly. Just put it behind the back seat and that should work. Thanks, and see you in a little while."

"*Senora*, this is too much," Isabella squealed. "You want me to identify the woman who killed Miss Ross and you also do not want me to go home. Where will I go?" She raised her hands in despair.

"I don't know, but I promise you'll be well-taken care of wherever you go. I will personally make sure of that." Marty stood up and started to gather her appraising items. "First, we need to go to the police station and have you see if the person my husband is arresting is the woman you saw murder Melissa Ross. Once that's done, I'll help you with the first steps of what will become your new life. Isabella, trust me, this will be the start of a fresh future for you, and a much safer one. Believe me, you are not alone. Many, many women have done what you are about to do, and all of them had very good lives because of it."

"I'm so scared," Isabella said, a solitary tear sliding down her cheek.

"That's perfectly normal. Get your purse and any other personal items you have. You won't be coming back here, because Tomas knows you work here. I'm sure the attorney for the estate can find someone else to cover for you."

*****

A short while later Marty pulled into the police station parking lot and saw a man waving at her. She waved back, turned to Isabella, and said, "It looks like my husband has someone waiting for us."

The man walked over to them as she and Isabella got out of Marty's car. "Hi, I'm Detective Bryant," he said. "You must be Detective Combs' wife. He sent me out here to wait for you. He wanted me to escort you in through a special security door that's not available to the public. Actually, you're the last ones to arrive."

"I have no idea what you're talking about," Marty said, turning to introduce her companion. "This is Isabella Lopez. Where do you want us to go and who else is here?"

"Well, to begin with, there's a beautiful white boxer that's here. I guess his name is Patron, and from what Detective Combs told me, your sister is calming him down. When the man, I guess he lives out at the compound with you, took him out of his car, the dog was growling and barking so loudly, no one wanted to get near him. Fortunately, your sister drove up just after they got here and was able to calm the dog down."

"I'm sure everyone was glad when that happened," Marty said. "He can be a little intimidating."

"You got that right. Anyway, the people who are here include some big guy, he's the one who brought the dog, your sister, and the husband of the woman we arrested for the murder of Melissa Ross. All of these folks, plus the dog, are inside the station in the viewing room. That's where we're going."

A minute later the detective unlocked a side door to the police station and led them to a room where the others were waiting. Patron was growling as he stood on his hind legs in front of a window, his guard hairs erect. Marty had been in the viewing room on prior occasions with Jeff, and she knew that the window was a one-way window. Laura was kneeling beside Patron, calming him. When

Marty walked over to him he turned and sat down beside her for a moment before resuming his stance at the window.

Prior to Marty and Isabella entering the viewing room, Jeff and the other detectives had taken Rhonda Taylor to an adjoining room that was visible through the one-way window. Four other female employees of the police department were also in the room. The other women were generally similar to Rhonda in physical appearance, were dressed in civilian clothes, and were about the same age as Rhonda.

The five women were asked to stand with their backs to a wall that faced the one-way viewing window. Each of them was directed to stand under a number that was painted on the wall behind them. Rhonda was standing under the number 3 that was painted on the wall behind her.

Detective Bryant escorted Isabella over to the one-way window and asked her to look at the five women who were standing against the wall in the adjoining room. He asked Isabella, "Do you recognize any of the women in the line-up as being the person you saw who murdered Miss Ross?"

Isabella looked at the five women in the adjoining room, turned to Detective Bryant, and said, "Yes. It is number 3. That is the woman who murdered Miss Ross."

Detective Bryant was holding a tape recorder in his hand and said, "Let the record reflect that the witness has identified the person standing in position number 3 in the line-up as the person she saw murder Melissa Ross. The person standing in position number 3 in the line-up is Rhonda Taylor. Miss Lopez, I want to be sure that I understood you correctly. Please say it again." He held the tape recorder about six inches away from her.

"The woman who is standing in position number 3 in the adjoining room is the woman I saw take a needle out of Miss Ross' arm, after she'd dropped to the floor. It is her. I am certain. She is the one who killed Miss Ross."

Isabella started shaking and began to softly weep. "I am so scared," she said. "I just know something bad is going to happen to me. That woman is going to come after me for what I've told you. Maybe she will kill me, too. What am I going to do?"

Detective Bryant turned off the tape recorder and said, "Miss Lopez, you can trust me. I promise nothing will happen to you. However, I do need to ask you a couple of questions, but first I need to tell Detective Combs that you identified Rhonda Taylor as the killer."

"*Si*."

When Detective Bryant returned from telling Jeff that Isabella had positively identified Rhonda Taylor as the person she saw murder Melissa Ross, he questioned Isabella for several moments regarding where she was when she saw the woman, how the woman had gotten into the house, how she knew Melissa Ross was dead, and other questions that would be part of the criminal case against Rhonda Taylor.

When he finished, he put his hand on her arm and said, "You did very well, Miss Lopez. Without your positive eyewitness identification, that woman might have gone free and murdered someone else."

Dr. Taylor spoke for the first time and said, "The someone else who might have been murdered is the woman I'm in love with. The woman I plan on making my wife. Rhonda is a very sick woman. I'm just sorry I didn't do something about it when I first suspected she was going insane. I will have to live with the fact I could have prevented a murder for the rest of my life."

Marty turned to the doctor. "Dr. Taylor, if it's any consolation, I met with your wife yesterday, and there was absolutely nothing that led me to suspect she was capable of murder. You might have thought she was having problems, but neither you nor anyone else could have predicted that a jealousy over something like being the foremost collector of art and antiques in Palm Springs would lead to murder. Please don't beat yourself up about it," she said.

"Thank you for those kind words, but the fact is assessing people's mental states is what I do for a living. It's ironic I missed that in someone I'd been living with for years. I guess the marriage was so dead I never really saw or realized what she had become. My personal distaste for my wife was such that I simply ignored her."

Marty looked through the one-way window and saw Jeff and several other detectives standing in the adjoining room where Rhonda Taylor had been taken. A smartly dressed man entered the room and walked over to Rhonda. They began to talk as Jeff and the other men left the room. A moment later, Jeff walked in the room where Marty and the others were.

Detective Bryant said, "Sir, as I told you, the lady, Isabella Lopez, identified Rhonda Taylor as the woman who murdered Melissa Ross. I have it all on tape. Here, you can listen to it."

Jeff walked over to a corner of the room, rewound the tape, listened to it, and then said, "Nicely done, Ricky. She's talking to her attorney right now. He's the guy who just walked in. I'm going back in there and will probably be interviewing her for the next hour unless her lawyer tells her not to answer my questions." He turned to Marty and said, "Why don't you take Miss Lopez home after she signs a few papers stating that we have the right to use this recording, if necessary, at the time of Rhonda's trial?"

"Jeff, I need to talk to you for a moment," Marty said in response. "Let's go over in the corner and talk." She told him about Isabella and Tomas and how she'd promised Isabella she'd never have to see Tomas again or have anything to do with him. When she was finished, Jeff pulled his phone out of his pocket and made several phone calls. When he was done, he turned back to his wife.

"Okay, Marty. We have a place for her. It's very nice and quite a distance from where she lived with Tomas. When I get through with Rhonda Taylor, I'll start the paperwork on getting a restraining order against Tomas that will prohibit him from contacting or being

MURDER & MEGA MILLIONS

anywhere near Isabella. Then we can begin the process of helping Isabella get a job and everything else that goes with something like this."

Detective Bryant walked over to them. "Sir, I couldn't help but overhear what you were saying," he said. "As you may have guessed, I'm very active in my church and helping women in Isabella's situation is one of the things my church is very good at. I don't mean to be disrespectful, but it probably has more resources than the police do."

Marty and Jeff exchanged a glance as Ricky continued to talk. "And as far as jobs, we have several very wealthy women in our church who are always willing to have women work for them who have problems like hers. As a matter of fact, we have a beautiful fully staffed high-security building for women who are in a situation like Isabella's. I'd be happy to make the arrangements for her and take her there."

Jeff looked at Marty for approval, and she nodded slightly and grinned. She was a sucker for burgeoning romances, and she sensed she was on the ground floor of one just taking off.

"Ricky, please go ahead with it," Jeff instructed him. "Marty, would you talk to Isabella and make sure that this is all right with her? It would free me up to make sure that all the i's are dotted and the t's are crossed in connection with Rhonda Taylor's arrest."

Next, Jeff walked over to speak with Dr. Taylor. "Doctor, you can leave and rest assured that your lady friend will be free from any future threats of harm. I know that you're going to have a lot of decisions to make regarding your house and everything else, but I think you can get started on making those decisions whenever you want, because your present wife won't be coming back home, period."

Wes Taylor shook Jeff's hand. "Thanks, Detective. This is a lot for me to process, but for the first time in a long, long time I feel hopeful about the future. I still feel somewhat responsible for Miss

Ross' murder, and I always will, but I'm sure time will help. By the way, I couldn't help but overhear your conversation with your detective about his church's ability to help women. If it's the one I'm thinking of, they're the best around. As a matter of fact, I think that church is the only one that has a facility like the one he mentioned. I've sent a number of my patients to them, and the support that was given to them amazed me. I'm confident Miss Lopez will receive the best help that's available." With that he nodded, got up, and walked out the door.

Jeff turned back to his wife with a quizzical expression on his face. "Marty, what is with everyone hearing what I was saying? I was speaking very quietly."

"Jeff, hate to tell you, but very quietly to you is a yell for anyone else. I just hope you don't talk when you're on a stakeout, or your days as the head of the detective branch of the Palm Springs Police Department might just be numbered."

Jeff's face fell. "I didn't know that. I'll make it a point to be even quieter in the future."

"Sweetheart, some things are impossible. I think that's one." She looked over to where Ricky was quietly talking to Isabella in Spanish and saw that Isabella was nodding her head in assent and even smiling occasionally. "Patron, Les, Laura, think it's time we headed for home. Laura, do you have to go back to the office or can you take the rest of the day off?"

"I think I need some time to decompress," Laura said, pressing her palm against her brow. "Between ghosts and psychic dogs, I'm exhausted. Meet you at the compound."

EPILOGUE

"John, I invited two people to join us for dinner tonight. I hope you don't mind," Jeff said as he strode out to the large table in the middle of the courtyard with Marty at his side. "You always have more than enough food, but I am going to put out some iced tea along with the wine. The young man I invited doesn't drink."

"Fine by me, Jeff." John grinned. "I love to feed people, and yes, I know I probably cook too much for us, but I've never heard any complaints about the leftovers," he said as he added two more place settings on the table.

"Nor will you," Jeff said, grinning. "Ever."

Marty turned to Jeff in surprise. "You didn't tell me you'd invited anyone to dinner. When did that happen, and who did you invite?"

"At work today. John's food is so good, I thought it would be nice to invite Ricky Bryant to eat with us at our compound out here. He's the young detective who was really instrumental in helping me solve the Ross murder case. Thought it might make him feel special. He readily accepted and asked if he could bring someone. I said sure, and then I asked who it was. Turns out he's seeing Isabella Lopez." Jeff raised an eyebrow and one of the glasses of wine John had poured for them at the same time. "You just never know, do you?"

"I didn't know that." Marty accepted the other glass of wine which Jeff handed to her. "I've called Isabella a couple of times to see how she's doing, but she never said anything about seeing Ricky. That's a nice outcome to a horrible situation."

"I think it might be serious," Jeff went on. "Ricky mentioned something about how they'd been seeing a lot of each other, which led me to believe they might be thinking of a future. He also told me she's working for a very wealthy woman who happens to have a number of antiques in her home, and was pleased to have Isabella work for her, because she wouldn't have to explain how careful she had to be with them."

"That's perfect," Marty said, taking a sip of her wine. "I'm really happy for her. She seems like a really nice person who got involved in a bad relationship with a totally unsuitable person and was in the wrong place at the wrong time."

The bell on the gate jingled, announcing visitors. Duke and Patron scampered towards it, eager to see who was there, followed by Jeff and Marty.

"Welcome," Jeff said as he led Ricky and Isabella, whose hands were entwined, into the courtyard. Jeff and Marty watched in amazement as Patron walked over to Isabella, sniffed her shoe, and then wagged his tail.

Marty shared a smile with Laura, who looked relieved, and then said, "Isabella, I think you've just passed an unwritten 'doggie likes you' test. Ricky, Isabella, I want to introduce you to my friends, including the best chef in Palm Springs."

RECIPES

BACON AND EGG BREAKFAST SANDWICH

Ingredients:
3 slices bacon, cut in half, widthwise
1 egg, beaten
1 hamburger bun (I like Sweet Onion Sandwich Buns by Van de Kamp's.)
2 very thin slices of onion (If you have a mandolin, use it to get these extra-thin.)
2 Tbsp. BBQ sauce (I prefer Sweet Baby Ray's.)
Cooking spray

Directions:
Lightly toast the bun. Place 2 paper towel sheets on a microwave-safe plate. Put the bacon on it and cover with 2 more paper towel sheets. Microwave on high for 6-7 minutes until crisp. Remove and place 3 pieces of bacon on each half of the bun. Lightly spray a 4" round ramekin with cooking spray and pour the beaten egg into it. Microwave the egg on medium for approximately 30-40 seconds, until slightly firm. (Be careful not to overcook. You don't want it to blow up!) Place the cooked egg on top of the bacon, add the BBQ sauce and sliced onion. Close the sandwich with the other half of the bun that has bacon on it.

NOTE: Microwave times vary, so keep a close eye on it!

CHOCOLATE TASTING PLATE

Ingredients:

6 chocolate bars (2 dark, 2 milk chocolate, 2 white chocolate)
2 small ramekins or bowls of dried fruit such as apricots, raisins, figs, etc.
1 small bowl of sliced green apples or other palate cleansers

Directions:

Break each chocolate bar into several pieces. Arrange the bars, dried fruit, and the apples on a large serving tray. Depending on the number of people you will be serving, you may wish to have a couple of trays.

ONE DISH SAUSAGE PASTA

Ingredients:

1 tbsp. olive oil
1 lb. sausage (I prefer the Jimmy Dean brand.)
2 garlic cloves, minced
1 14.5 oz. can diced tomatoes
8 oz. pasta (I like to use penne or fusilli.)
2 cups chicken broth (I prefer Better Than Bouillon.)
1 cup diced onion
½ tsp. crushed red pepper flakes
½ tsp. salt
½ tsp. pepper
½ cup half and half
1 cup Monterey Jack cheese, grated
½ cup green onions, thinly sliced

Directions:

Add olive oil to a deep skillet and turn the heat to medium-high. Add the onion and sausage and cook until the onions and sausage are lightly browned, about 5 minutes. Add the garlic and cook one more minute.

Add the chicken broth, pasta, tomatoes, salt, pepper, and crushed red pepper flakes. Stir to combine. Bring to a boil, cover skillet, and reduce the heat to medium-low. Simmer until the pasta is tender, about 15 minutes. Stir in the half and half and simmer until it is warm. Remove the skillet from the heat, add the cheese and stir until melted. Sprinkle with the green onions and serve. Enjoy!

SOUTHERN JACK AND COKE CAKE

Ingredients:
3 ¾ sticks butter, cubed (Always use unsalted. If you want it a little saltier, you can always add salt later.)
½ cup cocoa powder
¼ cup Jack Daniel's whiskey or any other good bourbon
2 cups flour
1 ½ cups Coca-Cola
1 cup sugar
1 cup light brown sugar, packed down
2 eggs
½ cup buttermilk
1 tsp. vanilla extract (Don't use imitation!)
½ tsp. salt
1 tsp. baking soda
½ chopped pecans
4 cups powdered sugar, sifted
Cooking spray

Directions:
Preheat the oven to 350 degrees. Spray a 9" x 13" Pyrex glass baking dish with cooking spray. Pour 1 cup of the Coke into a large saucepan. Add 2 sticks of butter, ¼ cup cocoa powder, and whiskey. Heat over medium heat until the butter melts and the mixture is smooth.

In a large bowl, whisk the flour, both sugars, baking soda and salt together. Stir the cocoa mixture into the dry ingredients and blend.

Pour the buttermilk into a small bowl, stir in the eggs and vanilla, add to the batter, and combine. Stir in the pecans. Spread the batter in the baking dish. Bake 30 minutes or until a toothpick inserted in the center comes out clean. (Ovens vary, so it may take longer.) Remove from oven and cool on a baking rack for 10 minutes.

In a small saucepan, melt the remaining butter with the remaining Coke and cocoa powder over medium heat. Beat in the powdered sugar, 1 cup at a time, until the mixture is smooth. Pour the frosting over the cooled cake and smooth with a frosting spatula. Let the cake cool completely before serving (I like to refrigerate it until about ½ hour before serving.) Enjoy!

STUFFED MUSHROOMS

Ingredients:
16 large white mushrooms
½ tbsp. butter
3 slices bacon, finely chopped
½ cup chopped onion
1 garlic clove finely chopped
1 cup shredded mozzarella cheese
½ cup soft breadcrumbs
¼ tsp. oregano
¼ tsp. Herbes de Provence
¼ tsp. salt

Directions:
Preheat oven to 375 degrees. Remove the stems from the mushrooms and finely chop. Remove the gills from the mushrooms and discard. Fry the bacon until crisp. Let cool and cut into small pieces. Melt the butter in a small frying pan over medium heat. Place the mushroom stems and onion in the pan and sauté until the onions are soft, about 3 minutes. Add the garlic and cook one more minute. Remove from the burner and add the remaining ingredients. Stir to combine. Spoon approximately 1 tsp. of the combined mixture into each mushroom cap. Press down gently with your fingers and shape

the top into a small dome.

Lightly spray a cookie sheet with cooking spray. Place the stuffed mushrooms on the cookie sheet and bake for 10 minutes. Plate, serve, and enjoy!

Paperbacks & Ebooks for FREE

Go to www.dianneharman.com/freepaperback.html and get your FREE copies of Dianne's books and favorite recipes immediately by signing up for her newsletter.

Once you've signed up for her newsletter you're eligible to win three paperbacks. One lucky winner is picked every week. Hurry before the offer ends!

ABOUT THE AUTHOR

Dianne lives in Huntington Beach, California, with her husband, Tom, a former California State Senator, and her boxer dog, Kelly. Her passions are cooking, reading, and dogs, so whenever she has a little free time, you can either find her in the kitchen, playing with Kelly in the back yard, or curled up with the latest book she's reading.

Her award winning books include:

Cedar Bay Cozy Mystery Series
Kelly's Koffee Shop, Murder at Jade Cove, White Cloud Retreat, Marriage and Murder, Murder in the Pearl District, Murder in Calico Gold, Murder at the Cooking School, Murder in Cuba, Trouble at the Kennel, Murder on the East Coast, Trouble at the Animal Shelter, Murder & The Movie Star, Murdered by Wine

Cedar Bay Cozy Mystery Series - Boxed Set
Cedar Bay Cozy Mysteries 1 (Books 1 to 3)
Cedar Bay Cozy Mysteries 2 (Books 4 to 6)
Cedar Bay Cozy Mysteries 3 (Books 7 to 10)
Cedar Bay Cozy Mysteries 4 (Books 11 to 13)
Cedar Bay Super Series (Books 1 to 6)... good deal
Cedar Bay Uber Series (Books 1 to 9)... great deal

Liz Lucas Cozy Mystery Series
Murder in Cottage #6, Murder & Brandy Boy, The Death Card, Murder at The Bed & Breakfast, The Blue Butterfly, Murder at the Big T Lodge, Murder in Calistoga, Murder in San Francisco

Liz Lucas Cozy Mystery Series - Boxed Set
Liz Lucas Cozy Mysteries 1 (Books 1 to 3)
Liz Lucas Cozy Mysteries 2 (Books 4 to 6)
Liz Lucas Super Series (Books 1 to 6)... good deal

High Desert Cozy Mystery Series
Murder & The Monkey Band, Murder & The Secret Cave, Murdered by Country Music, Murder at the Polo Club, Murdered by Plastic Surgery, Murder & Mega Millions

High Desert Cozy Mystery Series - Boxed Set
High Desert Cozy Mysteries 1 (Books 1 to 3)

Northwest Cozy Mystery Series
Murder on Bainbridge Island, Murder in Whistler, Murder in Seattle, Murder after Midnight, Murder at Le Bijou Bistro, Murder at The Gallery

Northwest Cozy Mystery Series - Boxed Set
Northwest Cozy Mysteries 1 (Books 1 to 3)

Midwest Cozy Mystery Series
Murdered by Words, Murder at the Clinic, Murdered at The Courthouse

Jack Trout Cozy Mystery Series
Murdered in Argentina

Coyote Series
Blue Coyote Motel, Coyote in Provence, Cornered Coyote

Midlife Journey Series
Alexis

Newsletter

If you would like to be notified of her latest releases please go to www.dianneharman.com and sign up for her newsletter.

Website: www.dianneharman.com,
Blog: www.dianneharman.com/blog
Email: dianne@dianneharman.com

COMING SOON

Murder at the Waterfront
Seventh Book in the Northwest Cozy Mystery Series
Pre-order and save $1.00
http://getBook.at/MATW

Men, Mobsters, and Murder! Poor Maureen. Was she just collateral damage?

This is the seventh book in the Northwest Cozy Mystery Series by USA Today and Amazon Chart #1 Bestselling Author, Dianne Harman.

Men loved Maureen, but was that why she was killed? She had an ex who wanted to reconcile, a chef she'd broken up with, and a salesman from Missouri who had fallen in love with her. Her brother-in-law had ties to the Mafia as well as some interesting business deals. Was she simply a pawn in their game? And what about Leslie, her ex-husband's fiancée? She wasn't too thrilled when Mac broke off the engagement to reconcile with Maureen. Plenty of suspects, but who's the murderer?

Al De Duco, a retired mobster, has taken over Jake's private investigation firm while Jake's helping a friend. Mobsters have a different way to deal with murderers. Sometimes they revert to old habits.

Join Al, his food critic bride, Cassie, and his Doberman pinscher as they hunt for the killer in this page-turning cozy mystery.

This is Book 7 in the bestselling Northwest Cozy Mystery series by USA Today and Amazon #1 Chart Bestselling Author, Dianne Harman.

Pre-order it now at: http://getBook.at/MATW and save $1.00

Open your smartphone, point and shoot at the QR code below. You will be taken to Amazon where you can pre-order the book.

(Download the QR code app for FREE onto your smartphone from the iTunes or Google Play store in order to read the QR code below.)